THE DEEP

BY MICKEY SPILLANE

MICKEY SPILLANE
THE DEEP

E. P. DUTTON & COMPANY, INC.
PUBLISHERS — NEW YORK

Library of Congress Catalog Card Number: 61-11267

This one's for Maury Riganto
in Norfolk, Virginia

THE DEEP

Long before I got there I heard the word. It seeped through the nighttime of New York, the tone of it muffled by the rain, yet strong enough to reach away out from its source to the far places of the city. It came to me in a gin mill called Hardy's just off Columbus Avenue from a half-bagged bim who had had the place to herself for too long.

She grinned crookedly when I walked in, throwing a half-sympathetic wink at my raincoat and then to the night outside. When I got my coat off she swirled the remains of her drink in her glass, threw it down and patted the seat next to her.

There's no sense arguing with that type. They move in anyway and it was easier sitting and buying than trying to shuck her off and it was too wet to go back into the night again. But, for an accidental partner, she was all right. Big, but they're better big. Harlow hair, bright white, yet soft and fluid like poured milk. And they're usually better blonde, too.

When she grinned again and fingered her empty glass I sat down and waved the bartender over to set us both up with the same.

She hoisted the glass in a toast. "Thanks, big guy." She

finished it off in one throw and sipped at the chaser with a smile of satisfaction. "Want to talk?" she asked me.

I shook my head.

"Now don't tell me you're feeling sad for that Bennett bum too."

The bartender tapped her arm. "You better knock it off, Tally."

"So what do I care about the bum? From a little hood he gets to be a big hood. All the way from a juvenile delinquent up. Look, Jocko-boy, that creep shook me like he shook everybody else and even if they did give the bum a five-grand funeral he's still a bum."

"Tally, damn it, you shut up . . ."

"Nuts. Nuts to you, Jocko-boy. Everybody else feels the same way. Every damn body is glad the creep is dead. Most are happy because he shook 'em and the rest are glad because now maybe they have a chance to drive the machine a while."

"I told you . . ."

"Okay, Jocko-boy, okay. Quit worrying. Who's listening? Only this guy here. You haven't got the joint bugged, have you?" She let out a giggle and reached for the chaser again. "So big Bennett is dead and all the little Bennett boys are crying. It's funny as hell."

This time she looked over at me and her eyes were beginning to film up. "Friend, do you know why they were *really* crying?"

"Tell me."

"First I want a drink."

Jocko-boy said, "She don't get . . ."

"Give her a drink."

He looked at me and his mouth got stiff. Then he reached for the bottle and poured one out. The bim grinned, winked and tossed it off.

"Now tell me," I said.

"Sure. I'll tell you. All the little stiffs and all the big stiffs from here to Brooklyn are bawling because they want Bennett's machine. Every mob in town is ready to rumble to grab it. The bucko-boys are loaded for bear and if you don't wear some kind of a badge you're liable to get shot for being an innocent bystander."

"That's not why they're crying."

"Easy man, I'm telling." She finished the chaser and nodded for another. "Trouble is," she said, "they're crying because they're scared to death of Deep."

I looked at her over my glass.

"You don't know who Deep is, huh?"

"Tally . . ."

This time I was the one who said, "Shut up, Jocko-boy."

She winked at me real elaborately. "Attaboy. Like I said, this Deep is a guy. He's a big man someplace. He's a bigger creep than was even Bennett, and mister, that's saying somethin'. Bennett and this Deep was like this, see?" She held up her hand with her fingers crossed.

"Who's on top?" I asked.

"Deep." She felt for her glass again. "Hear tell Deep was worse than Bennett ever was. Mean as hell. Carried a gun when he was a little kid. Only delinquent on the block with a real rod." She giggled again. "Tough boy, and now he's coming back."

"Yeah?"

"Sure, man. Him and Bennett were . . . something. Blood brothers, I guess. You know delinquents."

"Not altogether," I said. "They've changed lately."

"Ah, they're all alike. They're still bums. Bennett was always a bum and so's this Deep. They ran everything in shares when they were kids and took a crazy blood vow or something to revenge the other one if ever something happened. Boy, they were something then. They had the whole section organized and you know something? That was when Lenny Sobel was up top and he was careful not to get funny with those little kids. They could pull some pretty rough stuff."

"You have a big line on those boys, honey."

Her face flattened out. The eyes that had been filmy before suddenly cleared and for a second there was a bite in them. "That lousy Bennett got my sister on *horse* and she wound up a suicide at sixteen. I never forgot that. I was nine then. The pig. *The stinking pig!*"

She looked back to me again, the film shadowing her eyes. "This Deep. They say he was even worse. He pulled out a long time ago to let Bennett run that end. He said he was going to find something new to take over."

"Yeah?"

"Sure yeah, what else? He had the makings. Someplace he started creaming the suckers and some place he's the biggie. Now he'll be back." Her mouth twisted in a sneer and she laughed sourly. "In a way it's good."

"Why?"

"The boys won't rumble until they find out how big Deep really is."

"It makes a difference, huh?"

She looked at me and I was grinning.

"Sure, you jerk. If he's big they bump him, then rumble. Otherwise they rumble and get him sometime in between if he gets annoying."

"Why wait?"

Her mouth twisted up again. "No one knows how big Deep really is. Suppose he comes in with a mob?"

"That's not really the deal, sugar."

This time she smiled a little. "Smart boy. You're right. What they're scared to death of most is that they don't know what he looks like yet . . . and he just might be real kill-crazy. You know the kind?"

"I know the kind."

"So he blows in and does like he promised to do . . . knock off anybody one by one who touched his old buddy—Bennett. You know?"

I said, "I get the general idea."

"And maybe he can do it. Nobody knows. He's a . . . what's that stupid word . . . an . . . "

"Enigma," I told her.

"Smart bastard," she said. Then she glanced up at Jocko-boy at the end of the bar and laughed drunkenly. "Look at him. Face in a paper. He don't even want to hear about it. The laddies outside hear that I've been running off at the mouth to a stranger and they tell it to Jocko-boy the hard way. That right, Jocko-boy?"

He wouldn't look up from his paper.

"Now let all the delinquent idiots rumble. Let them all kill their damn selves. I'm glad as hell Bennett got it and I'll be glad when all the rest get it and no matter who comes first I'll still be laughing and when I can look at that creep Deep spread out on the sidewalk I'll spit on him like I did Bennett."

"Gal," I said, "that's hard talk."

"Don't call me 'gal,' damn it. That's what Bennett called me. Don't you or anybody ever call me that."

"I'll call you that, gal."

"Who do you think you are! Just because . . . "

"Deep," I said. "Call me Deep."

Jocko-boy kept staring at the paper, but he wasn't reading

it. There was a strained white look about his face and his tongue flicked across his lips a couple of times.

I finished the drink, put it down and looked at the bim. The cords in her neck were standing out tightly. "What's your last name, Tally?"

Her voice was a whisper. "Lee."

"Live close by?"

"On . . . hundred-third."

I waited.

"Over Brogan's market. Look . . . about what I said . . ."

"That's okay, Tally."

Now her whole lower jaw was quivering. "I . . . I run off at the mouth sometimes, you know?"

"Sure, I know."

"What I said . . ." she swallowed hard and bit into her lip.

"About being a delinquent? A creep? Better off bumped? You telling me you didn't mean those things, Tally?"

Then suddenly the fear was gone. The hardness and defiance came back and she said, "I said it. I meant it."

At the end of the bar Jocko-boy glanced back, startled.

I grinned at her real big. "That's the way, kid. If you say it, then mean it."

Her eyes went all funny looking. She studied my face for three deep breaths, then having decided, she reached for her glass and drained off what was left in the bottom. When she put it back on the bar she turned and stared up at me with tight, cold eyes and whispered hoarsely, "You're not Deep. You're too damn polite to be Deep. *He* would have splashed me by now. Deep never liked to be called names and he hated dames who talked too much like I just did." She took another breath, her eyes widening. "I can make up for having a big mouth, feller. I can pass the word that a phony's loose looking for trouble."

I nodded. "You do that. That would make everything real interesting then."

"Be glad to, big guy." Her mouth twisted into a wry smile. "Hell, man, if you were Deep you'd be packing a rod under your hand day and night just looking for somebody to shoot up. *Old Deep the cannon-boy* they used to call him. Too stinking tough to even bother hiding it. Carried the old rod where everybody could see it." Her eyes ran over me disgustedly. "You're Deep? Nuts."

I reached in my pocket for a half buck and spun it out on the bar. When I looked back at Tally her eyes were gone all wide and jumpy with fear and she couldn't take them off the spot at my side where she had seen the .38 in the speed rig.

I said, "Don't forget to tell 'em, Tally," and walked outside.

Wilson Batten had his office in the new building that had replaced the old Greenwood Hotel. The modern façade was a white smear in the darkness, the rain glistening coldly on the marbleized surface, an incongruous structure like a false tail on a dog.

A band of lighted windows girdled the second floor so I crossed over and pushed in through the full-length glass doors. On the wall beside the self-service elevator was a building directory listing all the occupants. Only the second floor was in all caps. It read, "WILSON BATTEN, AT-TORNEY."

Very simple. But this was a world where simplicity was a necessity. It was an asset in other worlds, too, where simplicity was really concealed arrogance.

I grinned, skipped the elevator and went up the stairs. In the foyer two girls were belting themselves into raincoats before a strip of mirror. One had a mouthful of bobby pins, so she nudged the other to take care of me.

"We're just closing," she said.

"Oh?"

"You waiting for one of the girls?"

I took my hat off and shook the rain out. "I hadn't thought of it. Should I?"

The impudent smile looked me up and down. "You wouldn't wait long, I don't think."

"I never have."

"No," she said, "I don't suppose so." The smile drifted away when I didn't move and she added, "You wanted something?"

"Wilse."

"Who?"

"Wilse. The Boss. Batten."

Her eyes widened in surprise. "Not now. You can't . . ."

"Now," I said.

"Listen . . . mister . . ."

"Now," I repeated.

Behind me the voice was soft, but had a bigness to it that was a quiet threat.

"Some difficulty, Thelma?"

"He wants to see Mr. Wilson."

"I see. I'm afraid it's much too late at the moment . . ."

I turned around slowly and looked at him. He hadn't changed much. Always the terribly efficient laddie who could make himself indispensable, but never enough genius to quite reach the top. One thing about Augie, though. He always was on the side of a winner. He could always tell them.

His eyes frowned, not his face. Something worked in his mind, like a mental yeast, but he couldn't finger it. For a second his shoulders tightened, then relaxed because that wasn't the answer, either. He was still the same Augie. He could still tell. He said, "You'll see Mr. Batten then."

When I agreed with a nod the two girls watched with amazement.

"Your name, please."

"Don't you remember, Augie?" My grin stretched a little. "Deep. Tell Wilse it's Deep."

Under his chin the cords of his neck strained against the collar. He remembered all at once, his brain settling into a new pattern of *now* and *later*, then he shrugged his huge shoulders under the tailored jacket and smiled. His voice had a pleasant rumble, an intonation of efficiency waiting to be utilized.

"I should have," he said. "But you've changed, Deep."

"We all change."

He stared at me hard. "You're bigger, somehow."

"Bigger," I repeated. "Good word."

The office I walked into was all mahogany and Gauguin. They hit you both at once and made you minimize the man behind the desk. He looked up, starched and creased, his hair thin across his head, but still dark. It's funny how few balding guys ever turned gray.

I said, "Hello, Wilse," and he pretended to recognize my voice.

"Deep." He stood up and extended his hand. "Good to see you, boy. Good to see you."

My grin ignored his hand. "I bet. I bet you're just overjoyed, Wilse."

His face was a professional mask but I knew what was happening to him. I pulled a chair up with my foot and sat down, dropping my hat on the floor. Augie reached for it and I said, "Leave it there." He stopped, threw a fast glance at Batten and stepped back.

"Old Wilse," I said, "the thief of Harlem . . ."

"See here, Deep!"

"Shut up when I'm talking, Wilse." I smiled and his eyes searched it for meaning. "You came a long way from the walk-up off Broadway. From old *Batty Batten* to Mr. Wilson Batten, Attorney. Pretty good for a thief, but not much different from a lot of success stories I know."

I shoved out of the chair and walked the perimeter of the room, studying each Gauguin in turn. Half were originals. The other half pretty expensive copies. "You did okay, feller."

"Deep . . ."

When I turned around and grinned Batten stopped with his mouth open. I said, "Batten, you're a thief. You're a scheming shyster who made good. You fenced stolen property once, you bought anything I could steal, you covered the boys pushing the happy stuff and were a good contact between certain parties and certain crooked cops."

"Several times I took you off the hook, Deep."

"You sure did, and you sure got your pound of flesh." I walked over closer and looked down at him. "I was a lot younger then."

"You were a punk," he challenged softly.

"But a good one. A tough one." I sat on the edge of the desk. "Remember Lenny Sobel? Remember the night the king and his court came to take you apart for a double cross and Bennett and I paid you off for all the favors? We put the big guys under a couple of guns and spit on them when they wilted. Sobel sent them back for us the next night and we sent him three shot-up hoods. Then I shot Sobel just for fun. Right in the behind. Remember that, Wilse?"

"All right. You were tough."

I shook my head. "Not really, friend. You know what I was."

"A juvenile delinquent."

"That's right. *Now* I'm tough." Then I grinned real big. "You know?"

The professional mask was back again. "I know," he acknowledged.

To one side Augie changed his stance. He was facing me now. There was more butter on my bread.

I said, "You have Bennett's will?"

"That's right."

"It's all in order?"

"I was his legal advisor."

"What does it say?"

For a moment he judged me, straining hard to see if I could be had. "Provisionally, you are his inheritor."

"What provisions?"

"First, that you arrive within two weeks after his death."

"This is the fourth day."

He nodded. "Second, that you satisfactorily determine his killer's identity in the event of violent death."

"Nice of him."

"He had great confidence in you, Deep."

"Was the word determine or avenge?"

"Determine. Mr. Bennett wanted it otherwise, but it never would have stood up. Legally, that is."

"Legally, of course. Now one more question, Wilse. Determine to *whose* satisfaction?"

"You are very astute, Deep." He opened the drawer of his desk, drew out a newspaper tearsheet and pushed it toward me. Outlined in red was a two-column, full-length spread titled "Uptown Speaking" by Roscoe Tate.

I didn't have to read it again. It was one man's hate being spilled over into print. A guy who couldn't make it the soft way crying out loud because others did. A guy who had a hate for three people in the world. Me, Bennett and himself.

"Prove it to Roscoe?"

"Not necessarily. Merely 'determine.' " A smile tugged at

the corner of Batten's mouth. "That won't be easy, you know."

"No, it won't. He hates me pretty hard."

The smile widened. "That's not why."

I looked at him quickly.

"Tate thinks you did it, Deep."

"Silly boy."

"But with reason."

"Go ahead," I said.

"The empire was a big one. You had been unheard from for twenty-five years. Could be that you knew where Bennett stood and decided to take over, figuring that he'd stick to the old agreement you two had of the survivor inheriting and . . . well, taking care of the . . . killer?"

"It's a killer, Wilse."

"You see how it figures."

"I see. Now tell me something. If I don't prove out, who gets the domain?"

His smile went into all teeth. White teeth very big and clean. "Me. I get it all."

"Smart boy," I said.

"Quite."

"I may have to kill you, Wilse."

He got pasty-white then. "You'd be tied into it so tight . . ."

"That still wouldn't stop me from killing you, Wilse. It would be easy. No trouble at all."

The slack in his face was that of an old man. For a minute he had forgotten what the real tough ones were like. In twenty-five years he had grown big to the point where sudden death had no personal meaning any longer, now he was staring it down again.

I said, "What do I come into?"

"Supposing I read the will. That should . . ."

"Tell me yourself, Wilse. You won't lie. I'm not worried."

His mouth was a fine, tight line, the tautness reaching up to his eyes. "The Cosmo Taxi Service, the old clubhouse building, several real estate properties consisting of tenements, lots, garages . . . I'll list them for you . . . half interest or better in four businesses and a brewery."

"Nice," I said. "Any cash?"

"Ten thousand upon appearing, which is now. All other monies and so forth when you have met the provisions of the will."

I held out my hand with a grin. Wilson Batten looked at it, then the grin, and let a hard smile crack through his lips. He opened the middle desk drawer, slipped out a yellow cashier's check and laid it in my palm. I said, "Last question. How long have I to meet the . . . provisions."

His smile had a nasty touch of laughter in it. "A week." All his teeth showed through it. "You think you can make it, Deep?"

I folded the check, shoved it in my pocket and stood up. "No trouble. Plenty of time." When I walked to the door I could feel his eyes on me and when I reached it I turned around and gave him a little taste of what he had to look forward to. I said to Augie. "Coming, friend?"

He didn't even look at Wilson. He said, "Yes, Mr. Deep," and walked out behind me.

Like I said, Augie was the kind who could always tell.

Roscoe Tate was the first kid on the block who had ever had a job. When he was fourteen he made the six-to-eight rush hour at the subway entrances with the two-star tabs and brought home more drinking dough for his old man. A year later he told the rumdum to beat it, called the cops to back up a nonsupport, wife-beating and cruelty-to-children charge, made it stick and supported the family from then on.

Now it was twenty-five years later and the papers he hawked once he wrote for now. The old man had drunk himself to death, the mother was in L.A. with a married daughter and Roscoe carried on a vendetta with the block he grew up on. The only trouble was, he couldn't make himself leave it.

He sat it out in Hymie's deli behind a chicken liver sandwich and a phone, scowling at some notes he had made. I walked in alongside the row of stools and pulled an antique chair out from behind the counter. Hymie looked up, his face squeezed mad, ready to cream anybody who'd touch his private throne, then froze solid.

When I slid the chair under the table and slouched in it Roscoe said without looking up, "You want big trouble, feller?"

I laughed quietly, and for moments it was the only sound in the place. Then his finger got white around the paper and his eyes rolled up to meet mine. "Deep," he said.

"Hello, Roscoe."

"You crumb, you got nine dollars and forty cents?"

"Why sure."

"Put it down." His forefinger tapped the table top. "Here."

"Why sure." I counted out the dough and laid it on his notes with a grin. A long time ago I had smacked him silly and lifted his weekly take out of his jeans. Now I laughed again when Roscoe picked up the cash and shoved it into his jacket pocket.

His face was pulled into tight lines and I could tell he was wishing that he was real man-sized for a change. "Don't spoil it for me, you bastard," he said. "I promised myself I'd take that dough back from you sometime."

"You want interest?"

"Don't be so stinking condescending." He licked his lips, tasting the beads of hate-sweat that had made a fine line under his nose. "I was hoping to take it off your corpse."

"Now you got it back, buddy. No hard feelings?"

"You louse. You miserable louse." He waited to see what would happen and when I grinned the malice hissed through his teeth. "So what do you want?"

My shoulders hunched in a shrug. "I don't know. Not yet. But it's *somebody* I want, Roscoe. You follow?"

"I got ideas."

"You know why I came back?" I asked him.

His hand wiped more hate sweat away. "Yeah," he said. "I think I know. I'll even talk about it because I hope I can get something on you that will hang you high as a kite."

"Then why?"

"You want the outfit. It's yours by inheritance. A whole mob of blank-faced idiots to go with it. A hand-hewn chunk of corruption and violence all set to roll into action. Brother, you and Bennett were some buddies, I can say that all right. You guys really stuck to the creed of the old gang. You make a blood pact and you sure keep it!" He stopped, his teeth an uneven line across his face. "So Bennett wills you the whole works . . . the buildings, the clubs, the dough . . . everything."

"Nice of him."

"There's only one hitch . . . you got to be louse enough to keep it."

I looked at him for a long time, the grin getting bigger. "You sure that's why I came back?"

"Yeah. I'm sure. You've been away too long for anything

else. It's big dough now. A million bucks and a tailor-made mob. *If* you can keep it. Murder's a tough rap and easy enough to prove."

I let the grin drop. "You little screwball, I didn't come back for any million bucks. I don't *need* any mob or any million." I stopped, then, "I didn't kill him, you pothead! You think I'd stick my neck out for that kind of stuff?"

Something happened to the expression on his face. The tenseness came out of it and there was an excited nervousness in its place. Roscoe said quickly, "Then *you* know where it is. Bennett left you that too."

I stood up and pushed the chair back to the wall. "Buddy, I came back for one reason. I want the laddie who bumped Bennett. Bad, I want him. You know?"

His voice was almost hushed. "I know." His mouth was a fine, tight line now. "That crazy kid stuff stuck with you. The blood crap. You want a kill, don't you?" He didn't let me answer at all. He said, "So okay, find him. I'm with you all the way. I hope you kill the pig so I can put the whammy on you. I want so bad to write your obit that it's coming out my ears. I'll help you find him, Deep. I hope you wipe out all the old pig crowd. Decimate the block if you have to. All the kids are growing up in Bennett's shadow and somehow I'm getting the feeling that you're even worse."

His chair skidded back and he stood up, his head tilting up into mine. "Tell me one thing, Deep. You're big where you came from just now. You're real big, aren't you?"

I laughed at him again. "Real big," I said.

His eyes flattened out. "Bigger than Bennett?"

"A lot bigger," I told him.

He accepted it with a nod. "I'll write your obit yet."

"That's okay. I'll even rough you in on background details as long as you help me find out who bumped Bennett."

"Deep, I'll be glad to. Happy is the word. Happy, happy. We get him, then you."

"You talking or doing?"

It was his turn to smile now. "You know me better. You were all bigger, but I don't scare. Not one damn bit. The pigs all know me and the way I feel. I'll blast hell out of them in my column anytime I can and they know it. So they lay off. You know the pigs. They figure me for an occupational hazard and anybody I tag deserves it. At the same time they're pretty cagy. I may come from the block, but this boy's no part of it. If they tag me they get bounced by the cops and hard or the paper steams things up something awful." His grin spread. "Bennett's gone . . . and now I think you'll be next. That'll be good."

I watched the pleasure of the vision creep into his eyes, watched him satisfy himself with a probing thought into the future. Then he said, "You inherited a lot of trouble, Deep. You'll never know."

"I inherited more," I said.

The notes under his hand balled up when he made a fist. His neck swelled into his collar and had a turkey-like color with the tendons standing out as if his head was Marconi-rigged. Still he tried to bluff it out. "What?"

"Helen. Irish little Helen. I understand I inherited her too."

Each word was a soft little thing. "I'll kill you myself if you go near her, Deep. Stay away, understand? Keep your filthy hands off the kid."

"Love, Roscoe? Distant affection?"

The curse he spit at me was even softer than his words.

I said, "She was Bennett's too. Now she's mine. She's part of the inheritance."

"You're going to be dead fast, Deep."

"Not by you, little man. You're too much a stickler for law and order. It might occur to you, but it won't happen. You'll wait for a slug or the law to get me and in between you'll die a little yourself. I hear she's quite a gal now. All big and beautiful like nothing else that ever came off the block. She was too young to deb in the old days, but I hear she's even better now. Hit a couple big shows on Broadway and got the slobs running after her. Yeah, Roscoe, she must be some doll. How come you're in love with her?"

His mouth hardly moved when he spoke. "I'm not. You just have a short memory, Deep." His eyes got heavy and dark. "She's my half sister, remember?"

I grunted at him. It was a point I had forgotten about. "I'll play it real cool, son. Just don't interfere or I'll twist you a little bit."

"Just like the old days."

"That's right." I looked straight at him and his eyes walked across my face, finding the scars and scratches that are the stamp of the jungle bred. He saw the rest of it too and let the disgust of it seep into his expression.

"What is it you want to know, Deep?"

"How did Bennett die?"

"You read the papers."

"That's right, but review me."

Roscoe shrugged. "He answered the door of his apartment and the killer popped him one right in the neck."

"With a .22," I added.

"Yeah, and close enough to give him a powder ring." He paused a moment. "A damn .22. A woman's kick."

His voice had a sneer in it. "Don't worry about your inheritance. Helen didn't pop him. She was rehearsing for a show that night."

"Where was Dixie?"

"He alibied out."

"That's what the papers said. Bennett sent him down for some Scotch. But how does it stand with you?"

"It was good. Bennett called him while he was at the place and told him to bring up a case of rye too. The guy there took the order and let his clerk go back with Dixie. They found the body together."

I said, "And everybody went for the picture."

"Yeah, and it stands, too. The guy at the liquor store added a new note . . . he and Bennett had a code word that okayed all calls, meaning that it was Bennett calling and not half the mob getting in on his booze bill."

"So Dixie was clear."

"He never was smart enough to dream up a thing like that."

"Then who got Bennett?"

"Ask the cops, sucker."

"They're too happy to see him dead to wonder much who killed him. Besides, I don't want information. I just want guesses."

Roscoe's face squinted up tight. "You know, Deep, I wish I did have a guess. I wish I had any kind of lead at all because I'd like to be around when you try taking the lid off."

"Off what?"

"Your inheritance."

CHAPTER III

The rain had started again; one of those slow, musty New York rains that has a meanness to it you can't quite define. It put a slick on the black pavements and gave the streets a sick, unhealthy glow.

I stood across from the hundred-year-old building that had been given a new face, but still smelled the same. The sign was new too. The old one had been hand printed, but this one was of neon, yet still read KNIGHT OWLS A.C.

Bennett always had been a sentimental slob, I thought. The old slogan . . . he'd stuck by it to the end. *Once a Knight, always a Knight.* There was no cutting loose, no drawing back. He'd owned the fanciest apartments and flashiest clubs in the city, but home base was the old spot where the Knights began.

From the beginning to the end, the difference was only a matter of three floors. The Knights had their beginning in a cellar. They graduated a flight at a time until they finally had the whole place.

And now, behind the carefully guarded grime that almost opaqued the windows, the Knights were meeting again. The king was dead. They'd be humping to find themselves a new one.

Those laddies had a lot to learn. They could stop humping right now.

The new king was here.

I crossed over to HQ and shoved the door open. It was the first time there was no squeal on the knob. In the old days a low buck drew that duty. You showed the sign or else.

The stairs still had the same carpeted surface. The holes were just bigger, that's all. There was a dip in the railing where Bunny Krepto had carved out a chunk with a switch-blade the night before he had been killed and up at the top of the landing the broken end had been worn smooth from hundreds of hands passing over the raw end of the break thousands of times.

I pushed the door open with my foot and it swung in without a sound. The guy at the post had his hands shoved in his jacket pockets, watching the to-do up past the bar at the rostrum, a butt dripping from his mouth and his eyes fogged up with hoople juice.

Like the old days, I thought. Nothing much had really changed. Instead of a pack of kids squatting on orange crates and old benches, the elaborate theater seats were filled with gray heads and big bellies and here and there you could spot the faces that had been on the front pages of the tabs the past year.

But their expressions were the same. Flat, unimaginative. But lustful, and that kind made up the best army to crowd out the rest. Benny Mattick was up at the microphone, his Brooklynese still unspoiled. Older and fatter, but still Benny-from-Brooklyn. Still the hot hoodman who had shot his way out of a dozen cop traps and the lad who had peddled a million in horse without ever having an arrest record.

Beside him was Dixie. I looked at the lank figure with the sunken cheeks, surprised that he was still alive and wondered how his arms had stood up under the barrage of needles that had juiced him into so many big ones. His pin stripe had a two-hundred-dollar look and the rock on his middle finger was worth a few grand uncut.

I stood there until the squeal spotted me and swung around with one hand yanking at his pocket. He stopped without getting his hand loose, grinning stupidly.

He said, "You got it?"

I didn't pull out the card they all carried now. I waited until he'd had a good look at me then peeled my sleeve back so he could see the old *K.O.* scars engraved on the back of my wrist by a knifeblade.

His face changed then. It was something that always happened to the new ones. That *K.O.* was prewar and wide enough to stay livid and each period was made with a lit cigarette butt.

I walked to the end of the seats and slid down beside the little guy and said, "Hello, Cat."

The double take was for real. "Jeez . . . Deep! When did . . ."

"What's up?"

"Jeez, Deep . . ."

"I asked you something, Cat."

"We're reorganizing, Deep. Jeez . . . Benny thought . . ."

"When did he take over?"

Cat swallowed hard, the spit having trouble going down. "Right when Bennett got it. Jeez, Deep. The club's big. You can't let things get shook."

I waved him quiet. From the stand Benny-from-Brooklyn was getting all wound up. He was nominating himself for king and from the look on his face it was all over but the shouting.

The Knights were big. They had loot. They were the protectors of the precinct. They were a political power that had need of a fine hand at the wheel and Benny was the man.

I looked around to see how the others were taking it, and it was still just like the old days. They didn't like it but they weren't looking for a showdown, either. They all had that bland, drawn expression that mirrored nothing, accepting what came for the time being, at least.

When Benny turned on his smile I knew the talking was about over. Next they'd take a standing, unanimous vote and go up to the bar for a beer. The others anticipated it too and shuffled in their seats.

Benny said, "Now . . . if there are no further questions?"

I got up and let the seat slam back. "I got something, Benny." Beside me Cat coughed nervously and tried to slouch down farther.

All those heads swiveled, frowned against the glare of the lights, squinted at this off-beat note. The murmuring started at the corners and swept inward like a gentle wave. Nobody wanted to be the first to call. At this stage of the game only the kings were on the board.

Benny had let it go too long. It got away from him and he knew it. He tried to stop it, but Dixie nudged him to silence and he said, "Who is that down there?"

I said, "Look hard and you'll know."

Then somebody said it from the far side. That one word and all the heads swiveled back fast. They got together in small bunches, passing it on, then Benny got it too. His face grew flushed and Dixie stood there like a stick with a kill-look plastered across his mouth.

When it was real quiet I said, "In case any of you new

slobs aren't familiar with the rules I'm going to tell you. Nobody's reorganizing anything around here. I'm taking over. Just like that."

Benny held onto the mike for support. "You watch it, Deep. You're not coming back here . . ."

"Come here, Benny."

You could hear the quiet.

I said it again. "Come here, Benny. Take ten giant steps and three baby ones."

Up on the little rostrum Benny took his giant step first. Then one more. Then down the stairs. Then he stopped.

"Right here, Benny. One more baby step."

The red was gone and his face had a pasty look. He was all tongue, trying to keep his lips wet down. He walked up in front of me and stood there. So nobody could miss it I did it real slow. I smashed him one across the chops with my open hand and sent him spinning into the wall with his eyes gone all misty.

Then I said, "Dixie . . ." and the squeal on the door gasped and beside me Cat edged down a seat.

Dixie didn't take baby steps. He came in the crabwise walk of his with a flat, deadly grin that meant he had a new hole in his arm tonight. He was flying so high he forgot there were still a few who weren't scared to death of the shiv he loved so well. I let him get close enough to kiss me off with his eyes, took the blade out of his fingers so fast he never knew I had it until I raked him hard over the ribs where the blood could make a mess for everybody to see. When I hit him his teeth powdered and he fell against Benny-from-Brooklyn and lay there sucking air.

I grinned at all the eyes. "Now you know the rules. This isn't exactly a democracy. It's more like a dictatorship and I'm the cheese. We hand it from one to another the way we like and when you think you're big enough to take over, then try. Just try. Be sure you're big enough, that's all."

When I looked around all the little pig eyes tightened in false smiles. Some turned away, some approved, some hated. But most were scared.

"Some things have changed the last few years," I told them. "I see new faces. Important people. I know why you're here and why you're connected. I'm hoping that none of you try anything spectacular because this kind of business is my kind of business. The organization will continue to move as it did under Bennett until I go over all the affairs. Now . . . any questions?"

A hand waved from the far side. "Deep . . ."

"Who is it?"

"Charlie Bizz."

"Go ahead, Bizz."

"You in for keeps, Deep?"

"All the way. If there are any other studs feeling hot to make it then you can choose up sides."

"Roger, Deep. Good to see you, kid."

I nodded in his direction. "Augie's picking up all the papers. Don't give him trouble. I want a roster of members and all the goodies that Bennett kept. Anybody holds out and there'll be trouble. Just like the old days."

The face that had been watching me without any expression at all grew a sneer. It belonged to a man whose physical strength was disguised by a layer of fat, but was visible in his eyes and the hatchet slash of his mouth. The sneer was cool, deliberately aimed and calculated.

I said, "Councilman . . . you don't look convinced."

Hugh Peddle who held the old Dutch district appraised me with a veiled look, never losing the sneer. His voice was soft, not like the sneer at all. "I'm just curious . . . , Mr. Deep."

"Are you?" I watched him carefully to catch any change in expression. "Beside you sits a Mr. Coppola. At the moment I understand he's a guiding force behind the incumbent party in City Hall. Do you know him well?"

"Quite well, Mr. Deep."

"You stout men are usually addicted to Turkish baths. Have you ever noticed the scars on his belly?"

"Often."

"Has he ever told you how he got them?"

"Never."

When I grinned his sneer twitched at one end and got hard to hold. "Ask him then," I said.

From three or four spots came grunts of acknowledgment and I knew some of the old crowd were still around.

The party wasn't quite over yet. There was still something left undone. I leaned on the back of one of the seats and looked out over the bunch. "Whoever killed Bennett better start running," I said. "I'm going to get him, and that's the end of his life."

Benny-from-Brooklyn and Dixie were standing now, their minds not fully accepting what had happened. Their faces went back twenty-five years, remembering the disgusting things that had happened below in the cellar and knowing that they were happening again.

I liked it that way.

Little Cat was watching me with that expression that got him his name. I waved to him. "You, Cat. Let's go."

He squirmed out with a happy laugh and waited. Like everybody else. They were all waiting too. I said, "You'll be hearing from me. Just sit tight."

The squeal opened the door with a respectful nod and we

went downstairs to where Augie was. The big guy looked at a speaker high on the wall and muttered, "Intercom."

"Then you know you're with me?"

"All the way, Mr. Deep. I know exactly what to do."

Cat opened the door and we stood outside on the street in the clean rain. He coughed into his hand and pounded his chest. When he could speak he said, "What's with me, Deep?"

"Like always, Cat. Up the walls and over the fences for you. In where no one else can go. The eyes, the ears."

"I ain't the same Cat any more, Deep."

"Trouble?"

"Lungs. T.B. But not so soon to kick it as you."

"Think so?"

"They'll get you, Deep. They don't want nobody as bad as they want you. They got big things doing for the squad. You'll only louse it. Couldn't you tell that?"

"I could feel it." I grinned at him, "Nobody was speaking up."

"You got the bull on 'em too quick. They ain't used to the old tactics. They're going grand these days. Big thinking. They don't do them cellar jobs no more. Man, you want to freeze them fat slobs . . . then bring up the old days down behind the furnace. Me, hell . . . it scares me too. I couldn't take that crap now."

"Neither can they, laddie. They like to smear it on, but that's all. Things have changed."

Cat laughed back. "Like I said, I'm with you. It won't be for long, but while it lasts I'm with you."

"You not scared of dying?"

"Man, man, I'm just scared of living. It's killing me." He grinned again and we took off down the street.

The cop on the beat had been old when I first knew him. Below the sweatband of his cap the gray was an insignia that meant more than approaching retirement. It meant a guy tough enough to stay around that long, one who knew all the ropes and all the rules, good or bad. In a way there was a determined finality in his stride, always that singular purpose of going ahead, never back. The hand that had swung a night stick for thirty years had lost none of its rhythm. The baton moved like a live thing on the end of the thong, its purpose immediate and deadly, a symbol no one could mistake.

He stopped in front of me and said, "I heard you came back, Deep."

"You know the grapevine, Mr. Sullivan. Travels fast."

"I also heard there's been trouble already."

"Not really."

His finger came up and traced a heart-shaped design a little to the left of center on my chest. "That's a vulnerable spot. Just a few grams of lead there and you're done, boy."

"You're talking like the old days, Mr. Sullivan."

"You're making like the old days, Deep." The wrinkles around his eyes seemed to freeze up. "Until now it's been quiet. Nobody's been shot up."

"Except Bennett."

"He wasn't worth much. Not more shooting. Nothing's worth that much."

"You've grown pretty philosophical since you whaled the crap out of me with a pair of handcuffs twenty-five years ago."

He nodded, remembering. "It didn't do much good, did it?"

"Some, Mr. Sullivan, some. I know the damage a guy can do swinging a set of cuffs. It won't happen again."

"Don't be too sure." His eyes went tight again. "You're in a big bind now, kid. Real big. You can start making the most of your days. There won't be many more."

I gave him a short laugh and looked at the hand that danced the night stick. His face went red and drawn and he said, "Still the wise guy. How many have you shot up, Deep?"

"Five," I said. "Five and two probables."

"Don't make trouble on my beat."

I shoved my hands down in my pockets and shrugged, "I'll try to oblige, old-timer. But if it happens, be careful. I have a sort of peculiar affection for you."

When I walked away I could feel all the little eyes that had watched follow me and knew the ears that had heard would pass things on. Maybe it had been a long time since trouble had touched the neighborhood, but those days were long gone now.

In twenty-five years the only thing that had changed in Brogan's market was the merchandise. The sidewalk was piled high with crated vegetables, obscuring the windows, and inside Brogan was still his same busy self in a tomato-stained apron and straw kady.

Beside the store front a narrow door led into a stairwell leading to the upper four floors, an almost opaque ascent where the bannister was a necessary guide. The second floor bell had a metal plaque stamped *Lee* but I didn't bother to push it. The way the stairs squealed and grated in those old tenements nobody came or went unannounced.

The second floor landing had two doors, but only the back one had a light behind it. I stepped over the cardboard cartons leading to it, skirted the row of bottles and gave the door a rap. There was movement inside, but no one answered. I hit it again and heard heels tap the floor. A barrel bolt grated and the door swung open.

Some things you can't get ready for. You can't get ready to meet a crazy beautiful dame in a cold-water flat. Not one almost as big as you are who's made all firm and round so you can feel the warmth that comes from her like perfume. You never can get ready for eyes that seem to taste you rather than see you, or black hair so alive the roll of it is a sensuous thing that makes you aware of buried compulsions.

I said, "Hi, sugar," and looked back at her.

There was an uptilting to her brows, a professional wariness. "Yes?"

"I'm looking for Tally Lee."

She shook her head lightly, making her hair swirl. "I'm sorry, but she can't see anyone. No one at all."

"Why not?"

"Tally has been sick. Now if you don't mind . . ."

I shoved the door open and walked in. "I mind," I said. When I closed it I walked toward the front into the bedroom where the single night light turned a pale yellow glow on everything and looked at Tally lying there on an old four-poster, her hair a harsh pink around an almost bloodless face. There was a deadness about her, the covers barely moving as she breathed.

I said, "What happened?"

"Sleeping pills."

"Why?"

"Something scared her."

"She all right now?"

"For now, maybe," She sucked her breath in hard. "So get out, man."

"When I'm ready." I kept looking down at Tally.

"Now, man," she said. "Otherwise you can get hurt." From behind she could see me shake my head. "I can't get hurt," I told her.

"Don't fool yourself, man. Maybe you don't know who I am."

I waited a long moment before I said, "I know who, kid."

Either she didn't hear me or didn't care. "Lenny Sobel is my . . . friend. He doesn't like guys like you. I can tell him."

I turned around and tilted her head up with a finger under her chin. "Then tell him from me he's a slob. Tell him I have a chubby little slug I'd like to blow up his tail and if he gets in my way I'd be real happy to show him how it works. Anytime. Anywhere."

She batted my hand away with her eyes spitting at me. "Who'll I say is calling, man? Who wants to get killed that fast?"

I grinned and watched those full lips pull away from a lovely row of teeth in an almost animal snarl. "Can't you remember good?" I asked her. "I pulled a rape artist off your back once and creamed a pair of the Bello mob who tried to shag you in a cab. I took a hell of a shellacking from a five-and-ten manager who thought I lifted his junk when it was you. Remember now?"

She tried to press back into the curtains, her breath caught in her throat. She was all eyes, looking at me carefully, trying hard to ease the rigidity that was on her like a sudden freeze.

"Deep . . ."

"Yeah. Your memory doesn't go back very far, Irish. Hardly at all."

She pressed the back of her hand to her mouth. "Deep . . ."

"You can still say it nice, kitten."

It came back to her in small pieces; the street, the gang, the kid stuff in school. The roof where we leaned against a warm chimney and two children walked through the virginity of love with a first kiss.

Then she remembered it all, and other things too, until it showed in the hardness of her face. "You were better off out of mind, Deep."

"That seems to be the general opinion all over." I grinned, let my eyes search her completely, then: "You're a good-looking dame, Irish, though that isn't much of a change. You always were."

"I know."

"You should. It's pretty obvious." I knew when I had quit smiling. I said, "You got it working for you too, haven't you? Lenny is up there these days."

Her hand was a streak aiming for my face but it wasn't fast enough. I caught it, threw it down and held her tight against me. "Don't try that again, kid. Nobody touches me without getting bounced and I'd hate for it to be you. Don't figure that punk Lenny and me to be in the same class and if you want to put yourself on his level then be damn nice to me. Damn nice, understand? I'll belt you cockeyed as fast as look at you if you ever get funny with me again."

There was a breathless quality in her when she said, "You're off it, Deep. You're dead and buried already."

I nodded. "So I've heard, only I won't be the first there, and therein lies the rub."

Her eyes arched up at me.

"Everybody hates to get killed," I said. "Nobody quite wants to be hero enough to go first."

I let her go and she drew back, rubbing her wrist. "You stink, Deep." She said it quietly, disgust plain in her voice.

"What happened to Tally?"

"I don't know. She called me earlier and was slightly hysterical. I figured she was drinking and told her to go to bed. When I came by she was in a chair, out like a light with half a bottle of shoo-fly gone."

"You called a doctor?"

"Naturally. He was here all morning."

"Nothing serious?"

"Not physically."

"Why did she call *you*, Irish? You're an uptown broad. You haven't smelled this neighborhood since you were twelve. You're as out of place here as a hat on a horse."

"You stink, Deep."

"Now you're talking neighborhood again. Talk uptown and answer me, damn it."

She pulled back, a frown across her face. "All right, I'm uptown. But I had one friend in my life."

"Not Tally."

"No, not Tally. Her sister." She saw me studying her and shook her head. "You don't remember her. Girls didn't mean that much to you then. She was my age and we were in the same class. You know what happened to her?"

Tally had told me that herself. I said, "Yeah, Bennett got her hosed up. She flipped."

Muscles and cords made tight lines in her neck. "Off a roof she flipped. She killed herself." Her smile was deadly and hard. "That was your friend who did that."

"So?"

"So you stink, Deep."

I slapped her across the mouth with the back of my fingers and watched the red seep into her face. "Stay at ease, kitten. With me, stay at ease."

It was almost as if I hadn't touched her. "You're tough, aren't you?"

"Real."

"Mind if I stick around and see you get killed?"

"Not a bit."

"I'm going to enjoy it."

"I'll try to put on a good show."

"Of that I'm sure. And I'll help you. I'll try to get you killed just as hard as I can."

Her arms reached up and went around my neck and that warmth I had felt at the door wrapped around me like an oven and her mouth was a tantalizing, wet kiss of death, a quick fiery thing that was hello and goodbye in one.

When she drew away she glanced down at the bed. "Why'd you come?"

"You wouldn't understand," I said.

"Try me."

I took a check out of my pocket with Tally's name on it and showed it to her. "A grand."

"Hardly worth her sister's life."

"You stupid dame, it isn't compensation. It's payment for information."

"What makes you think she'd give it to you?"

When I glanced at her she almost backed away. "Because she's like you," I said. "She wants to see me killed too. She'd give me anything I wanted to get me killed."

"Not anything."

"But you would," I said. "You'd give me anything."

"That's right. Just so I could be sure it would get you killed." Her breath was coming too fast and there was a hot depth in her eyes.

I wrote a short note, clipped it to the check and put it on the empty pillow beside Tally. When I looked up I said, "I'll see if I can't arrange it that way. Come on."

Downstairs I found a neighbor who, for twenty bucks, would stay with Tally, and a doctor who, for another twenty, would look in on her at intervals. A quick call to Augie got me a guy who would stake out the house and make sure everything went okay.

When I came out of the phone booth Irish was waiting, nicely tucked into a mink that did nothing to disguise the contempt she felt when she had to look at me.

But that was okay too. It's more fun catching a mouse than playing with one and she was some mouse.

I steered her outside, waved a cab over and nudged her in. I told the driver the name of a club and leaned back. Irish looked across the seat at me, the contempt clouded by curiosity. "Why all the business with Tally?"

"Because anybody who hates so hard is bound to have something I can use," I said.

"Use for what?"

"To find Bennett's killer."

"A very noble crusade."

"And you want me to get killed."

"More than that, remember? I want to be there to see it happen."

"Aren't you afraid you'll get sick?"

"Maybe, but it will be worth it."

"Why?"

"Because I hate too. I hate just as hard as Tally. I hate whatever turns little kids into filthy, immoral things who can turn on their own kind for something like money or power. I hate the political lusts and greed that drive decent people to the wall so one person can be big. I hate that so hard I could spit and that's why I hate you."

"And yet you're Lenny Sobel's . . . friend?" There was contempt in my voice now.

"It's a point you probably couldn't understand," she said, "but I'll tell you anyway." The corners of her eyes drew up in nearly oriental points. "By being his . . . friend, I can exert enough influence to make it easier on . . . some people."

"And maybe rougher on others?"

"Maybe."

"Have you ever forgotten the night on the roof by the chimney?"

"No."

I grinned to myself.

"But that doesn't stop my wanting to be there when you get killed. I'll give anything to see it happen."

"Anything?"

She nodded earnestly. "Anything."

CHAPTER V ————————————

When they tore the guts out of Fifty-second Street, one of the bistros was overpaid for expediency's sake, changed its name from The Kickoff to The Signature, and with a small move north and the perversity that belongs only to New York, became an overnight bang and by now a two-year success story.

It had good food, smooth music, premium beer and whisky and top prices, and you still needed reservations even for lunch unless you were big enough to bandy Lenny Sobel's name around and make it stick.

When we got out of the taxi, Irish Helen's face was beautifully quizzical, not so much at me as at herself, not knowing whether to stick it or run out.

I overtipped the driver a buck for luck, took her arm and started toward the door.

She said, "You know where you're going, don't you?"

"Sure," I nodded. "Your boy's place. Maybe you'll sound off and he'll be hot for my head."

"Smart guy. You're real smart, Deep."

"I've been told already."

"Yeah." Her eyes were real cold. "You should be scared stiff, man. You should be shaking in your shoes."

I stopped with my hand on the ornamented handle of the door. "You ever see me scared, sugar?"

"Maybe not in the old days."

"You won't see me now either."

"So you're a big one," she said flatly.

For a couple seconds I just looked at her, then nodded. "Everybody's asked me that lately. I told them, so I'll tell you too. Yeah, I'm a big one. They never saw anyone big like I am."

The frown creased her eyes again. "How did you know this was Lenny's place?"

I grinned at her. "I'm a big one, remember?" I opened the door and eased her through.

The headwaiter was an impeccable Slav imported in '49 from Paris by the *Galveston* and lately lured to The Signature by the big buck. His name was Stashu, he wore two hero pips in his lapel for underground activity in the last war and a nod of recognition from him could put you on the smart list in anybody's book.

Others were standing in the lobby, a few accepting cocktails on the house from a pretty waitress. Some of the junior exec types waited their time at the bar, preferring the side lines of the main room to the ignominity of just waiting.

I handed my hat and raincoat to the kid in the checkroom and turned back to Irish Helen. She was tall and cool, feeling everyone's eyes on her and playing it just right. She was waiting to see what happened next and waiting to laugh when it didn't. I walked to the plush chain where Stashu was quietly talking to a waiter. He looked up, smiled and nodded, lowered the plush chain and led Helen and me to a table and discreetly removed the reserved sign that had somebody else's name on it.

He took our orders personally, smiled again and left.

Helen looked up at me, something like a shadow across her face. "That went too nice, Deep."

"Of course."

"You've never been here before." It was a flat statement. I just looked at her and waited.

"How'd you work it?" she asked.

"Headwaiters are paid to know people. Everybody."

The shadow left her face and now I could see the tight lines of indecision that touched her. "He'll tell Lenny," she said.

"He'd better."

The drinks came then, timed flawlessly to make lunch the thing that it should be. Twice Stashu stopped by, inquired with his flavored English if everything was all right, and left happily when assured that it was. At two-thirty the lunch music faded into cocktail hour numbers, the room partially emptied and Lenny Sobel made his appearance.

He was fatter now. Still greasy looking, but able to wear five-hundred-buck suits and a ten-grand ring with an air of authority.

Lenny Sobel never walked fast. It might have been that he couldn't. It might have been that he didn't want to. He neither walked nor strolled. It was sort of a *step* that he took. He made it hard for the two who walked behind him. They had to either stop a moment then catch up or quarter the area at a slow pace merely to stay abreast.

He reached the table, smiled a fat smile first at Helen, then smiled a fat smile at me.

I said, "Hello, pig," and if it weren't for Lenny's fast hand wave I would have been shot right there and the two boys back of me on somebody else's kill list.

But I knew the slob would wave them off fast and my

grin told everybody I knew it. I said, "Make them come around in front, Lenny."

His smile was still there. It was a friendly smile, bunching the fat under his eyes into humorous lines. He brought them around in front and they stood there docilely, just waiting. If Lenny said kill . . . they'd kill. Right now he said to stand. So they stood.

One was a TV western type, tiny-hipped and overbroad at the shoulders where his jacket was cut to carry a rod. The other was as average as a person can get. I nodded to them both and in order said, "Harold . . . Al. Good to see you."

Only Al, the average one, flicked. I said, "Your buddy's a Q and Dannemora grad, Al. Lousy partner."

Lenny Sobel's hand touched my shoulder. "You know my associates?"

"Sure. Great guys. Al's the smart one, though, and you got to watch him. Not a rap to his name and looking to go places."

The hood looked at me steadily, nothing showing in his face this time.

Sobel asked, "That right, Al?"

"I work for you, Mr. Sobel. You know what I can do."

Lenny's smile broadened. "You ever meet this man, Al?"

"Not yet, Mr. Sobel. I think I'm going to like it if you want me to introduce myself."

The fat wreathed itself into a laugh around Lenny's mouth. "Deep?"

"Go ahead," I said. "For fun why not pull the cork and let me shoot all three of you. First you, Lenny, then these two *schmarts* in order. It should be fun. Go ahead, pull the cork."

Helen's voice was a hoarse, *"No . . . Deep!"*

The two hoods came in a step.

I said, "Tell them for me, Lenny."

They looked at him and watched his fat smile fall apart. Lenny said, "Let it drop."

Al started, "If you want, Mr. Sobel . . ."

"Let it drop, Al," he repeated softly. "You and Harold wait for me outside. I'll be along."

He waved again and they left, then pulled a chair out slowly and sat down. "You shouldn't be too carefree with those boys, Deep."

"They different?"

"They're different."

"I'll find out soon for sure and tell you, Lenny."

"You seem to know them pretty well already."

"I get around good. Anybody to know, I know. You know?"

His smile was getting tired now and he glanced over at Helen. "I see we've recaptured old times."

Her eyes picked up a strained look. "Lenny . . ."

"Perfectly all right, my dear. When a man is impetuous as is our old friend Deep, one can easily get caught up in his backwash."

It sounded funny coming from him. I said, "Picking up class, Lenny?" I grinned when he stared at me. "It's better'n the old days now. Then you were just a hood playing angles. Now you got class. Polish."

"You're looking for trouble, Deep."

"I'm expecting to get it, Lenny."

"You will. You came back for trouble, didn't you?"

I leaned back easily in the chair and from any place in the room you would think it was just a nice friendly conversation. I said, "I didn't have to come back for trouble, buddy.

I had plenty of it where I was and I sat on top of it and squashed it without any sweat at all. Not any." I tasted my drink again, swirled it in the glass and put it down. "You know why I came back, Lenny."

"Tell me."

"I'm taking over."

"You think?" His smile had angry tics at the corners.

"I already have," I told him.

He started to come out of the chair, his pudgy fingers tight around the arms, squeezing into the wood. The cords of his neck rippled under the fat and only the thin edge of his teeth showed between his lips when he spoke. "*You little punk. You street-corner bum. You lousy little cellar rat . . .*"

Real softly I said, "Remember when I shot you in the behind, Lenny?" Something in his eyes said that he did. Very well. "There were people looking then and I didn't give a hoot." I stopped and grinned again. "There're people here and I still don't give a hoot."

He seemed frozen in that half-standing position until I pointed for him to sit down. He let his breath out, sat down and his composure came back slowly. He almost seemed ashamed of having thrown his bit.

When he was ready he said, "You didn't come here just to eat, Deep."

"That's right. It's more of a visit. I'm seeing all the boys, the big ones, the little ones, all the laddies with the dirty, sticky fingers. I'm letting them know what they got coming and they better get in line. I came here to tell you that I have your operation pretty pat in my head and if you have any ideas about coming aboard you'd better figure on doing it with your hat in your hand."

He shook his head in wonder at what I had said, his eyes

searching my face to find a chink in my attitude. "You've thought this thing out?"

"Not especially. Not until Bennett got killed."

"You amaze me, Deep."

"I shouldn't."

He bobbed his head earnestly. "But you do. Here the organization is bigger than it ever was. It reaches into every phase of politics and commerce and has fingers to reach out overseas if it wants to. It has millions to buy and sell what it wants and you're taking it over, just like that."

"Just like that," I agreed.

Lenny folded his hands together on the table and leaned forward. "Tell me, Deep, what makes you think you can do it?"

"Because I've been thinking."

"Like what?"

"How another punk like Bennett was able to do it."

He tried but he couldn't control the sudden gasp. The lines worked in his neck again and made a lie out of his soft smile. "Your . . . erstwhile partner was an organizer."

"Sure."

"He was tough. He shot his way in. He was lucky, too. He intimidated the right people exactly at the right time. He had a brutish nature about him that made killing a pleasure, and a childish lack of responsibility that made him a terrible sort of person."

"I'm embarrassed. You're analyzing hoodlumism to which I've devoted my career."

"Don't laugh about it, Deep."

"I'm not, feller. I'm just curious about the other reason."

His face darkened. "What other reason?"

"The one you haven't told me about yet."

I stood up, waved to Stashu and handed him a bill to more

than cover things. "Let's go, Irish. Our pudgy little friend here will now carry the news to all the biggies who haven't already heard."

Very deliberately I looked down into Lenny's porcine face. "Tell them straight, chum. I'm in. I'm on top. If I yell jump they ask how high and if I say spit they ask how much. Anybody goes after my skin gets gunned down fast and if there's any doubt about who makes the try I'll rack up a couple of big fish just for samples. Meantime I'm finding out who bumped Bennett. It's not going to be a hard job and it won't even be a long one. But it sure will be fun when I find him. Or her. I'd kind of like it to be you, Lenny. I haven't shot you for a long time, have I?"

The collar was too tight around his neck now, cutting in so deeply his face was suffused with red. "I won't even have to touch you, Deep. The chair'll get you. The first time you put the heat to somebody, even if it's a Bowery bum, you'll get fried. You're marked, Deep. You got that smell of frying around you right now."

"You lost your class talk, Lenny. Let's not fall back into character at this late date."

"Get out," he hissed.

"Coming, Irish?"

Without looking at her Lenny said, "She can stay if she likes."

"Uh-uh," I told him. "She doesn't dare. I might get killed without her watching and she'd never forgive herself. Come on, Irish."

"It would be better if you stayed," Lenny told her.

She shook her head, her eyes cold and serious. "I'm sorry, Lenny. He's right. I want to be there when it happens." She picked up her purse and shrugged her magnificent shoulders into her coat, then stepped ahead of me to the aisle.

Behind us Lenny laughed with genuine humor, a soft, furry kind of laugh.

Outside the rain had started again and the taxis cruising past all had the flag down. I took Helen's arm and edged along the buildings out of the wet and started walking toward Sixth Avenue. We crossed over, headed south until we reached Martin's and went in out of the drizzle.

There wasn't anybody in the place except the bartender, a thin, graying man with Broadway-wise eyes who nodded hello, brought out two coffees on order and withdrew to the end of the bar to watch TV.

I spread my change on the bar, picked out the dimes and told Helen to hold tight. Her answer was the same cool stare of disgust, with her face mirroring the anticipation she knew would be realized.

My three calls took as many minutes and when I went back to the bar I finished my coffee. When I put the cup down she said, "Where away now, big man?"

I said, "Did you ever make bread?"

Her eyes caught mine in the back bar mirror. "A long time ago."

"Remember how yeast worked?"

Only her eyes were visible over her cup and they seemed to take on an upward slant. She nodded without speaking, finished her coffee and called to the bartender for a refill.

The guy who came in had little mouse eyes and a limp mustachio. The peak cap was a throwaway and a little too big and his pants and coat were alley stained and smelled sourly of sweat and garbage.

I said, "Hello, Pedro," then waved to the bar stool next to me. "You want a drink?"

"No. No drink."

"Money?"

"No. I want nothing from you. I just come here. What you want?"

"Sit here."

"I don't sit."

I reached out, lifted him by the arm and sat him on the bar stool. "You sit," I said. When I looked at Helen the lushness had left her mouth and she was hating me again. I grinned at her. "He's the kind of people you like, Irish? He's the kind you use your influence to protect?"

"Keep going, Deep. You're doing great."

"Thanks, baby. I'll keep on trying. I want you to be overjoyed when I get killed. Our friend Pedro here is an important man in the scheme of things. That right, Pedro?"

"I don't know how you talk." He held his hands bunched into fists close to his belly.

"What are you doing to him, Deep?"

I shrugged noncommittally. "Nothing. It's just that Pedro is going to tell me a story. You know the one, Pedro?"

He shook his head nervously.

"So I'll clue you, Pedro. I want to hear about how you found Bennett when he was killed."

Helen's cup stopped halfway to her mouth. Pedro's hand began to twitch so hard he had to hold it with the other. He shot a quick glance toward the door and when I shook my head his eyes rolled piteously and he seemed to shrink down inside his clothes.

"I . . ."

"Go on, Pedro."

"I don't know this thing you are saying. I don't know . . ."

"Okay, man. Then we stop playing. Suppose I put it this way. Feel in your left-hand pocket."

Instinctively his hand dropped to his side, felt the contents of his coat and in that one second he got the picture and tried to jerk away. I grabbed his arms, made him hold the edge of the bar and watched him while he shook.

Helen said, "What happened to him?"

I grinned nastily so Pedro could see it. "Nothing special. I just put our buddy in the path of law and order. He's a junkie, so I dropped a few day's popping in his pocket with the gimmicks and if he gets picked up he goes cold turkey downtown. In five minutes a cop'll walk in here and off this laddie goes. Unless he talks, of course. In that case he can even keep what's in his pocket."

The distaste of it made Helen slide away from me. "There are names for people like you," she said.

I nodded. "So I hear. Now let's listen to a speech. You got maybe four minutes left, Pedro. You can have it any way you want it."

"You no tell?"

"I don't have to tell, friend."

"This one . . . Bennett. I did not keel him. He was already there. You understand?"

I nodded again.

"He was already very dead. This you know? I did not keel him. He had one very big hole here . . ." he tapped his throat where the neck joined the body. "I take his watch. It was not a very good watch. For it I got one dollar. I take his wallet. He has twenty dollars. In his pocket he has ten dollars. That is all I take. I sell the watch. That is all. I run away. I do not think anybody knows this."

"Where's his wallet?"

"I throw it someplace."

"Like where."

"I think I know."

"You get it, Pedro. You find it and bring it to where you live and keep it there until I come by. You understand this?"

His head bobbed again. "Si. I understand. You know . . ." he hesitated.

"I know where you live," I said.

He started to say something else, stopped and slid off the stool. His departure was noiseless, like a shadow leaving. When the door closed Helen looked into her cup, the puzzle plain on her face. "Bennett was found dead in his room," she said.

"That wasn't the first time he was found dead."

"How did you know?"

It was the same question Pedro almost asked.

"Only one person in the world could get close enough to Bennett to shoot him in his own house," I said.

"Who?"

"Me, sugar. He always had a pathological fear of relaxing his eternal vigilance in his own place and getting creamed on his Persian rug. It was one of his little foibles."

"You called it real smart, Deep." Her tongue ran lightly over her lower lip. "You had an inside track?"

"No . . . just a reputation. The watch had an engraving on the back and he sold it to a Scorp who knew what it meant."

Her hand stopped me. "What?"

I said, "I boosted that watch from a department store in '32 and engraved the back *To Ben from Deep*. It was a cheap job, but he always liked it. The Scorpions are a punk

club on the other side of Amsterdam Avenue, but they knew
what those words meant. The kids are on it all the way.
Junkies have a bad habit of blowing off at the mouth when
they're flying and he let the bit leak out. Like I said, it
reached me fast."

"How did you hear of it?"

My eyes started to squint up. "The ties that bind," I said.
"Even the punks have their heroes. Bennett was one. I was a
dark horse, but still running."

"But never the police. They didn't know about this," she
said sarcastically.

I looked at her disgustedly, "You're forgetting your early
upbringing, kiddo. You weren't hothouse raised. That block
was your block as well as it was mine and you had your
fingers in a few pockets for pennies. Don't make me recite
times and places. Those punk kids wouldn't give the cops the
right time and you know it. To their own personal heroes
they'd run off, maybe, but not to cops."

"Who was your hero?"

"Dillinger," I said.

"It figures," she said seriously.

The bartender came down and emptied the Silex in our
cups. He fingered the change out of the pile and went back
to the other end, those funny wise eyes of his a little too
all-knowing.

Ten minutes later the big guy came in. There was a stiffness in his walk and the way he held his hands. To keep
them busy he opened his raincoat and shoved them in his
pants pocket. The steel glint from the twisters and handcuffs at his belt showed briefly, spelling out what he was if
you couldn't already tell from his face. He didn't look at her
when he said, "Beat it, lady."

Without a word she got up and went down the length of the bar to the ladies' room.

I said, "You got it?"

His fingers flipped two folded sheets from his jacket pocket, handed them to me, then snapped together impatiently.

"Easy, buster. Relax." I opened the sheets, took my time about scanning them, deliberating over each word, then when I was finished reached in my coat and slipped a C note from the roll. I handed it to him longwise and his fingers ate it up, but not fast enough for Helen to miss the business before she sat down again.

She held her breath until he had gone, then let it out with a tiny hiss and cut me to pieces with those eyes again. She said, "Pay-off," very softly and all the hate for the putrid system of things was in her voice.

My voice had an edge on it too. "Sure, kitten, but that's the way things get done. You want to know something, you force it or buy it. I can do a little of each, but one way or another I get what I want."

"Always?"

"All the time, Irish, and don't damn well forget it."

"What was it this time?" The corners of her eyes had that Asian look again.

"Very little. Just an official police report on Bennett's death." I slid off the stool, stood up and buckled my coat. The bartender eyed the change I left on the bar, nodded his thanks and I took Helen's arm and led her outside.

While we stood in the doorway waiting for a cab I could feel her watch me, feeling for words. She said, "Deep . . . where did you come from?"

"Why?"

"Because you're part of this mess and rotten clear through.

You know all the angles, all the answers. Filth and nastiness are too familiar with you. You walk down the street and every eye that sees you knows you're not like other people. You're big and mean and lousy and have death written all over you. I wonder who you are and where you came from."

"Yeah?"

A sneer touched her mouth, spoiling its lushness. "I heard about Bennett's will too. You had to arrive within two weeks. His death made national headlines so you would have heard about it right away. Still, it took you four days to get here. Where is four days away from here, Deep?"

I waved a cab down instead of answering her. When I closed the door I told her to check on Tally and stay there until I called her. Just as the cab started to pull away I had one second to see her eyes go crazy wide and snapped my head to one side so that my shoulder took the full impact of the sap that would have torn my head open.

My whole right arm was totally paralyzed, but I didn't need it at all. He had the sap up for another shot when I kicked him into a sprawling mass.

Down the street Helen's face was a white oval in the back window of the cab, so I waved at her, stepped on Al's working hand so the fingers snapped and walked across the corner to an empty cab waiting for the light to change.

Behind me a woman let a scream wail out and started yelling for the police.

CHAPTER VI ————————————

The apartment building where Bennett died belonged to me. Provisionally. It was far from the best that he had owned, but sentiment had kept him chained to the street and he had gotten some strange kick from remodeling the shabby tenement so that on the inside it had all the earmarks of Park Avenue.

While I waited for Augie I looked down the block that had spawned Bennett and me and the others and wondered why it was that it never seemed to change. The smells were the same and the sounds were the same. Diagonally across the street was the place I had been born and the guy hunched in the doorway nursing a bottle of beer could have been my old man. I looked up at the roof and the niche was still there in the parapet where Bennett and I had pried up the bricks to throw into the middle of the Crowns when they came up from Columbus Avenue looking for trouble. Almost automatically I glanced down to the base of the street lamp where two of them had fallen, smashed senseless, their blood staining the sidewalk, remembering the police cars and the ambulance and the wild, heady flight across the rooftops. It was a very special night because it was the first time we had ever been fired on and it made us pretty big men on the block. George Elcursio who had run with the Vernon mob in Chi had seen us the next day and gave us the big buddy wink for our brashness. A week later he had us doing odd jobs for Sig Musco's end of the Syndicate operation and we had our first taste of what power meant and what money could do.

Augie didn't interrupt the brief reflection. He waited, patiently. When I turned around he handed me a set of keys in a wallet. "Mr. Batten was rather reluctant about letting me have them, Mr. Deep."

"You talked to him?"

His smile was faint. "I talked to him. I'm afraid you have him pretty badly upset."

"The worst is yet to come, Augie lad." I started across the street to the apartment, aware of the fact that we were far from unseen. Little would ever happen on this block that went entirely unobserved. Here for hundreds of eyes was a macadam stage, lit by day and night, where an unending living drama unfolded against a backdrop of stark reality. Here the play was a timeless tragedy, life realistically portrayed, death always an impending thing ready to step from the wings on a gunshot or knife-slash scream cue. And always in their places, watching intently so as not to miss one facet of the show, was the audience. Sometime they came so close as to be a part of it themselves.

At the stoop Augie said, "They held a police guard on the place until yesterday. Two patrolmen, one upstairs and one here."

"Routine," I said and he nodded agreement.

We went up the worn flight of stone steps to the door and I opened the lock, went in and switched on the light. Even though I knew what to expect it came as a surprise. There was nothing of the tenement squalor left. Even the outlines of poverty had been altered and you felt as if you had been transplanted suddenly to a place far downtown with the park or the river outside your door. The walls and ceiling were gleaming white, touched faintly with gold trim, original contemporary oils framed in wormy chestnut lending color to the whiteness.

The stairway was gone completely. In its place to the rear was a small self-service elevator. It was a cute trick, I thought, like a modern style tree house where you could pull your ladder up after you. I wondered how he got past the building inspectors.

Augie showed me the way in, holding the door open to the lower front room. Again, the decorator's touch was evident. The room was striking, comfortable, but not lavish in the taste that Bennett would demand if he intended to use it often. Evidently this was the place where certain persons could be met, briefly entertained and kissed off without introducing them to the privacy of personal quarters. Bennett had gone a long way. A real long way.

I said, "What's the general layout, Augie?"

He took in the room with a sweep of his hand. "This is nothing here. Three rooms used mainly for business. He kept a bartender and a maid here more or less permanently. Mr. Batten let them go when . . . it happened."

Before I said it Augie shook his head.

"They could tell you nothing. They were sister and brother. Both congenital deaf mutes. It was one of Mr. Bennett's precautions."

"Smart. I didn't think he was that smart."

"A lot of people made that same mistake, that's why they lost out to Mr. Bennett."

"Really?" I swung around and grinned at him with a touch of sneer thrown in. "How come you didn't attach yourself to Ben, Augie?"

It didn't ruffle him at all. "When Mr. Bennett was fighting his way up it would have been a good deal. But when he reached the top he wasn't at his best trying to hold on."

"He did it quite a while."

"As I mentioned . . . only because he was smart."

"What did Batten have?"

"Mr. Batten is shrewd. At this stage he had an edge."

"There are tough ones around, Augie, who could take old Wilse as easy as spitting."

"Perhaps, but those will wind up dead too soon. Calculating the odds and including life expectancy, Mr. Batten was by far the best opportunity for me."

"Until I came along, you mean."

"Exactly."

"Now let's have the straight pitch, Augie."

He knew what I meant and smiled, his hands behind his back rocking gently on his toes. "You'll take the tough ones, Deep," and this time there was no *Mr.* "You'll edge out the shrewd ones and do just like you and Ben planned twenty-five years ago. You'll have it all in your hand for just a little while and then it will be gone. If you were just going after the king's throne you could do it, but your primary cause is to find a killer. You'll get him, Deep, but in getting him you'll die too. If the state doesn't get you a bullet will."

"You think you could take me, Augie?"

He shook his head and smiled broadly. "I won't have to."

"And after I get it?"

"Then I'll take over. When you get finished there won't be anyone left to oppose the move. I'll be the only one left who knows the entire operation by then anyway."

It was such cool thinking that you would never imagine this guy to have clawed his way out of the sewer slums to make it this far.

I said, "Supposing I can hold it after I get it, Augie?"

His smile broadened. "That's all right too. I still can't lose. I'll be close enough to the top and you'll be the target."

"You have it all figured out."

"That's right. I have it all figured out."

"Meantime you're my boy so show me the rest of this layout."

At the elevator the signs of the Homicide Division were plain. The obvious places a person might touch showed traces of print dust, and areas of activity were marked by clusters of cigarette butts ground into the floor.

At the first landing we went through a poolroom, a well stocked bar and a library. The police hadn't bothered to conceal the obvious fact that they had gone through the place. All the signs were there. Nothing had been missed and whatever they were looking for hadn't been found or never had been there at all. Even the pool table had been moved to search the sections under the feet.

It was on the third floor that Bennett had lived. And died. It was here that the stamp of his own personality was evident. The decorators had had a different thought in mind in the beginning, but it was a thought Bennett couldn't live with. The touch of the tenement was here, not that it was introduced, but that it had never left. The garish plush furniture in tasteless maroon was Bennett's choice. The two imitation ebony lamp bases had an erotic motif and nearly every piece of furniture had an autographed nude photograph, suitably framed, decorating it. The bar was overly mahoganied and overly chromed. The combination TV and record player was outsized and scarred at the edge from carelessly laid cigarettes. I studied it from every angle, a strange feeling of familiarity touching me. I shrugged it off and walked across to the desk.

Beside it part of a body outline in chalk marred the polished flooring. I said flatly for no reason, "The police found him here."

Augie sensed something. "He died there."

"Not here," I told him. "They just found him here."

He frowned at me, then his eyes went to the dark brown stains that matted the rug and the mess by the door and the bloodied handprint on the wall.

I took the copy of the police report from my pocket, went over it carefully, then handed it to Augie. "They think he got it inside here. He thrashed around while he was dying and messed the place up. Their opinion is that a guest was responsible."

He never took his eyes from the sheet. "Nobody could get that close to him. Besides, any entertaining he did never took place up here."

"You've been here, Augie. You aren't new to this room."

He still didn't look up. "Twice when Mr. Bennett had an illness he needed legal work done. I was the liaison agent between him and Mr. Batten. He had a gun beside him all the while." He finished the report and handed it back.

"Bennett died in an alley up the street," I said. I filled in the details except for saying who Pedro was and watched him while he thought it over.

It didn't make sense to him, either.

I said, "Augie . . . why did they want him dead?"

"They . . ."

I cut him off with, "Not who, Augie. Why. Why did Bennett die?"

"He was pretty big, Mr. Deep."

"I know."

"The big guy is always the target."

"Why, Augie?"

"I can only guess," he said.

"So guess."

His hands folded together again. "Talk has it the syndicate is growing."

"Bennett was in."

"Mr. Bennett was a scared man. The syndicate seemed to find it . . . impossible to deal with scared men."

"You're reaching for it but you're not hitting it, kid."

He teetered on his toes again and stared down the empty expanse of the room. "Suppose I give you my opinion in an illustration. Mr. Bennett was one, who instead of controlling the team with a slight touch on the reins, preferred, instead, to jerk them whichever way he wanted to go." He stared at me steadily a moment, then added, "It's only an opinion, of course."

"Of course. But there's only one thing wrong and you know it as well as I do. This was no syndicate kill. Their method never varies. The outside boy who never sees the payee, the big blast and so-long. They're not going to pop him off with a .22 and they're not going to hit anybody in the neck from two feet away. You know how many professional kills are still unsolved locally?"

"I know of a few."

"This isn't one."

"It could be," he said quietly.

"This was eyewash? A red herring?" I shook my head. "No dice, friend."

"The word has been out a long time."

He was feeling again. I said, "They could be getting smarter. I hate to give them that kind of credit, but it could happen. A nice sloppy job with some gimmicks thrown in could really mess things up for the cops. The only hitch is that the cops don't know Bennett didn't die here."

"In time they could find out," he said.

"But who's that smart, Augie? Who wanted Bennett dead that badly?"

Augie smiled again, his eyes glinting. "Why, Mr. Deep, everybody wanted Mr. Bennett dead."

"Enough to buy a kill and leave a possible chink in the armor?"

"I think so."

"Or was it that somebody hated him that hard?"

"It could be that too." He smiled again. "Nobody in the driver's seat is ever liked."

I nodded and made a tour of the room again. I went into the bedroom for a cursory look around, then into the bathroom and back to the kitchen. The place had been searched. Thoroughly. The police shook the place down the first time, but somebody else had done it too. I called Augie in and pointed to the scratch marks on the floor where the refrigerator had been moved out and back.

"What do you make of it, Augie?"

"The cops didn't do it."

"No . . . they wouldn't go that far."

"What would fit under or behind a refrigerator?"

The thought was plain. Augie shrugged and frowned. "A kilo or two of H could make it, but Mr. Bennett wouldn't keep it around."

"He was in the business, wasn't he?"

"Only second-hand, I understand. He did business with those who were in the business."

I said, "There are two other possibilities. Jewels or cash."

The frown deepened between his eyes and he shook his head again. "No jewels. He never fooled with that market. Neither was it cash. We handled all Mr. Bennett's accounts and he declared everything to keep out of the Treasury boys' hands. He was investigated every year but was absolutely clear. No, it wasn't cash. He never did a cash business. Within the statute of limitations he was clean, clean."

"So I'm missing a bet."

His eyes sought mine. "Evidently."

"Don't be smug, Augie. It'll come."

We went back to the living room and just stood there, looking. Finally I said, "Why is this place so familiar, Augie? There's something here I can't quite latch onto."

"Can't you tell?" he said. "Can't you remember back?"

"I'm trying."

Then I got it. The plush, the maroon, the incongruity of everything. "It's like the old cellar club, isn't it. Make this stuff old and worn, toss some dirt around and use candles instead of lights and you got the old K.O. clubroom."

"That's right."

"A real sentimental slob," I muttered.

"No . . . just no class."

There was no doubting the sincerity in his voice. Augie had come a long way and he knew just where he was headed, but now his opinions were showing the influence of his attitude. He was big and he was hard, but he wasn't kill-toughened and this one little thing kept him a step behind the leader. So far.

"I'll be staying here from now on, Augie. Make sure everything is in order. You know, phone, groceries. And get somebody in to clean up."

"It's been taken care of already, Mr. Deep."

Before I could answer him the phone rang and I lifted it from the cradle. I said, "Yeah?"

And Cat's clipped voice on the other end said breathlessly, "Deep? Good. Look, I just spotted two boys I knew from Philly. Lew James and Morrie Reeves. They hire out and they come expensive. They checked in at the West-hampton under the names of Charles and George Wagner and after they went to their room I slipped the doll at the PBX a bill to listen in to their calls and the only one they made went to a public phone and the guy on the other end brought you into it. Said you were in Bennett's place."

"How'd you know it was an outside phone?"

"Hell, I could hear all the racket. Sounded like a subway booth."

"Could you spot the voice?"

"Jeez, Deep, I couldn't. Look, you better blow, man. Them cats are hot for your skin. These boys got a wild rep, you know?"

"So have I, Cat."

For a few seconds he was quiet. "You want me to stick with them? If you want I could pull something that could make these cats scat like crazy."

"Let them go. They won't be in too much of a hurry. They'll make themselves nice and comfortable first."

"Well, what should I do? Man, you're being set up!"

"So come on over and have a drink. We'll talk about it later."

His voice was a tired whistle and he hung up. When I put the phone back I told Augie to round up a couple of the old crowd to stake out the place and then beat it on home.

He made the calls there, picked up his hat and waved so-long. I waved back and watched him get into his car from the front window, then I turned the TV on, sat on the floor and waited for Cat.

Twenty minutes later the chimes went off, I pushed the

buzzer to open the downstairs door and listened to the hum of the elevator climbing up.

There was a single sharp rap on the door and I yelled to come in, then looked around. But it wasn't Cat. It was Councilman Hugh Peddle and his two friends were well dressed hoods who went along under the title of "advisors."

Rather than get up from the floor I waved to the chairs and said, "Sit down, laddies, sit down. You'll have to excuse the informality. I wasn't expecting anyone."

Hughie's eyes sneered back at me. "It'll only be a short visit, Deep."

"Oh?" I could feel a nasty grin pulling at my mouth. "How'd you find me?"

"You left a wide path, Deep. You were leaving yourself open to being found, but don't think you're being clever."

"You came to tell me this, huh?"

"Not exactly."

"So?"

"How much will you take to leave town?"

I inched back slowly and leaned against the sofa. "I'll collect a million or so by sticking around, pal."

"Only if you meet the terms of Bennett's will."

"You mean to sell out now?"

"Not at all. Let Batten have what there is. Keeping it and managing it is nothing but a headache. You take a cash settlement and leave. The sum will be quite substantial."

"Leave to where?"

"Wherever you came from. Wherever you want to go. Just leave."

"Who's got that kind of dough?" I asked.

"Never mind. It's there and there's no catch to it. The money can be deposited for you, handed over in cash . . .

any way you prefer. No rough stuff afterwards. You get to keep the money."

"That's a real nice deal, Hughie."

"Well?"

"I like it here."

The smaller of the two hoods smiled gently, as if he felt sorry for me. His mouth never moved when he spoke. "If you want, Mr. Peddle, we can push this bird a little. It's not hard to make them reasonable."

I said, "Tell him, Hughie boy."

The Councilman got all red in the face and I could see his beefy shoulders hunch under the coat. He made an impatient motion with his hand and turned back to me again. "What about an outright sale then. The price will be above anything you can make in a lifetime and you can keep Bennett's junk too."

I timed it so he wouldn't know I was reaching. "What's there to sell, Hughie boy?"

He didn't trust himself to speak. There was rage in his face but fear in his eyes and before the wild anger of the moment could make him point the finger I looked at the two hoods and said, "Either one of you even twitches and I'll pop one right between your horns."

A tic pulled at the mouth of the taller one, like he was trying to keep from laughing. "You can't be that fast," he said. He kept watching my hands where the thumbs hooked into my belt. He was wondering how long it would take to make a cross-draw to a shoulder holster.

I said, "I know how you can find out."

The red left Hughie's face and he said, "Stop it, Moe. He's got the rod on his belt."

The hood sucked in his breath at the mistake he almost made and let his face go blank. Then the small one chuckled.

"From the floor he'd be your only hit, friend. What do you think I'd be doing?"

Behind him Cat said softly, "You'd be dying, chump," and when the guy turned around he looked down the barrels of a shotgun and went dead white. Hugh Peddle touched them both, turned and walked out. The elevator whined again and I watched them climb into a car on the street below.

When Cat lowered the hammers of the shotgun and propped it in a corner I said, "Who tipped you?"

"The stakeout across the street."

"What'd you do, fly in like Peter Pan?"

He laughed like a little kid. "You forgetting the old Cat, Deep? Up the fire escape and in the window. Like fog. Remember that poem?"

"About the fog coming in on little cat feet?"

"Yeah. Well, that's me. And you better be the same, you feel like staying alive."

"The imports?"

"Them is right. I made a coupla calls and got a confirm on the target. It's you. Five G's apiece across the board."

"I come expensive."

"You don't know how much. They also got another five G's to split between them from another source to hold up the play for a few days."

"Screwy," I said.

"Yeah." He craned his neck to look at me squarely. "You ain't shook, Deep?"

"Nah." I waved my thumb at the couch. "Let's sack it out a while."

"Sure, Deep. Mind if I have a drink first?"

"Help yourself."

He walked over, opened one end of a cabinet and

brought out a bottle. One drink started him coughing until he almost collapsed, then he straightened up and wiped his eyes. I said, "You know your way around here, Cat?"

"Natch. Ben used me for a mailman. He never used the phone when he wanted orders passed around. Why?"

"No reason. Let's hit it."

He rolled on the couch and I headed in to the bedroom. As I got to the door Cat asked, "Suppose those guys drew and I wasn't there, Deep?"

"I would have popped them between the horns, buddy."

"You think?"

"They wouldn't be the first ones I popped," I said softly.

CHAPTER VII ━━━━━━━━━━━━━━━

At seven fifteen Cat came in and shook me awake. He lit a butt, sucked in a drag and stood there coughing his lungs out for a couple of minutes. He tried it again, but it wasn't any better so he squashed it out.

I said, "You have long, Cat?"

His shoulders hunched in a bony shrug. "I died a long time ago, Deep."

"Get off it."

"No kidding." He squinted down at me. "My time was up two months back. It's all gravy now."

"No chance for a cure?"

Cat shook his head. "Maybe last year, but what the hell? What difference does it make? You know, I ain't even got a bucket to kick. If I had, some crumb would swipe it anyway." He grinned at me and coughed into his handkerchief again. "This world isn't worth while living for or dying over," he said. "Everybody's money hungry and trying to kill each other off like crazy. The lucky ones get it early and it's over with. The rest have to sweat it until something catches up with 'em. Me . . . maybe I'll be one of the lucky ones."

I sat up in bed and stretched until my shoulders cracked.

I climbed out, looked at Cat and shook my head. "So be a fatalist. Drop dead."

He laughed and it started him hacking again. When he stopped he rolled his handkerchief into a ball and left the room. I heard the toilet flush, then he came back. "You know, Deep . . . the only sorry part is that I'm starting to have fun again. Like the old days, remember?"

My face started to tighten up. "Were they really fun, Cat?"

"I don't know. I never knew anything different. Sometimes I wondered. The old man whaling the crap out of me, never enough to eat, hardly a week without getting your head almost knocked in. We had our kicks, though."

"Remember the club from Ninth Avenue who gave that dance?" I asked.

"When those goons tried to shag Helen and Sugar Lee down the cellar? Sure I remember that. Man, how we tore that place apart. Hardly nobody walked home that night. I got six stitches in my back from that one. You and Bennett beat hell out of that cop who tried to break it up."

"He busted my nose," I said.

"You stole his rod, too, so it evened things up. You still got that rod, Deep?"

I pointed to my pants hanging on the closet door. The .38 in the speed rig weighed them down, pulling them out of shape. I said, "Go call Augie and get him over here."

"Sure, Deep." He was halfway out the door when he stopped and turned around. "You know, them days weren't really so much fun."

"Yeah," I told him. "I know. Then we were all punks. *Now* we're going to have fun. We'll make up for it."

Augie had some details of the operation with him. The

package was small, but the scope of the organization a vast thing that swept like the smear of a giant hand across the city, poking fat fingers into Jersey and outlying sections.

I went over the sheets quickly, getting a synopsis picture of Bennett's empire, estimating the take and the angles. I spent a couple hours making notes for my own reference, then stacked the sheets and put them back in the folder.

I handed them to Augie. "Anybody give you any trouble?"

"No. They might have wanted to, but no one did."

"Good. Where's the breakdown on it?"

"Mr. Batten has it in a safe place. It's available any time we need it."

"Or want it," I said.

"Or want it," he repeated.

"I don't suppose Wilse likes the idea."

"He hasn't much choice, has he, Deep?"

"None. You think he's holding anything back?"

Augie shook his head. "He can't afford to. Mr. Batten isn't exactly the . . . violent type. He doesn't want trouble. I think he'd prefer to wait you out."

"He's remembering something you're forgetting, Augie." He looked at me, puzzled. "All Bennett's trinkets will come to me by law. Me or Batten. But you don't inherit an empire of policy slips and horse rooms and whore houses and protection that goes with it. You take it. It's up for grabs and the biggest one takes it. *I* got it now."

"That's right, Deep. All you have to do is keep it."

I gave him a nasty grin and nodded. "It won't be hard."

At noontime Hymie's deli around the corner sent up lunch. There was a paper on the tray turned to Roscoe Tate's column of "Uptown Speaking" and I knew how it got there. The lead paragraph was the first step in building

my coffin, the gentle whisper of hate, the feathery touch of
fear.

Murder has come back to Manhattan. The death of
"Boss" Bennett had the crime hierarchy scrambling for
control of his multimillion dollar enterprise of filth and
corruption. But they were too late. A dead man had left
his hand in office. The Heir Apparent had been selected
long ago and has taken command. The Deep One is back.
Murder is with us again.

When I read it I handed it to Cat. He grimaced and said,
"Wise guy. You want to learn him one?"

"It's bad enough he has to live with himself, Cat."

"He always was a punk. Him and his chicken liver sand-
wiches." He flicked his eyes up at me. "Saw him give a dog
half a sandwich once when a hungry little kid was standing right next to him."

"Dogs got to eat too," I said.

Both of them looked at me, their faces impassive. I said,
"I'll speak to the boy myself. That sticks and stones bit
don't go with me."

Augie said, "Play it smart, Deep. You don't want to fight
the press."

"I don't? Why not? What do you think the press can
do? So they call me names. They put on the heat. So
what?"

"It's not quite like the old days," he insisted.

"I know, pal. It's improved, if anything."

Augie squirmed a little in his chair. "Tate doesn't pull
any punches. He's not like . . . us. All his life he worked
hard. He peddled papers and clerked in the office until he
finally got his name in print. He sweated. He's not an easy

guy to push around. It's been tried and he blew the top off things. You get him going and he gets pretty damn mad."

"I've seen him mad before, feller. Remember, Cat?"

"When you lifted his poke?"

"Yeah."

Cat chuckled at the memory. "Tried to shoot you. He grabbed a piece off Frankie Carlo and tried to shoot you. Boy, I can still see you flipping over that railing into Morgan's basement." He laughed again. "How come you never blasted him after that, Deep?"

I grunted and shoved back in my seat. "Hell, I had it coming, I guess. Couldn't blame him. Anybody did it to me would've had a split head quick. Funny thing, when I slammed that door in his face he just laid there and cried like a damn baby. I could hear him bawling, then that stinking Sullivan picked him up and took him home. I bet his old lady browned out when he went home with a cop."

Augie said, "You were lucky you didn't get creamed."

I laughed at him. "Hell, he didn't even come close. Besides, he got his money back. Nine bucks and forty cents. It was the first thing he asked for when I saw him the other day."

"You're pressing your luck, Deep," Augie told me.

"Yeah, well let's go press it some more."

"How?"

"We're going to see Benny-from-Brooklyn and his buddie Dixie."

"You're crazy," Augie said softly.

I nodded. "Natch." I grinned at him. "But first let's talk to our newspaper friend."

Hymie was too busy at his counter to talk and told us that Roscoe Tate was probably still at home. I left Cat

there to hold him in case he came in, walked two blocks
down and turned the corner to where Roscoe still lived in
a tenement apartment and posted Augie at the door while I
went in.

Unlike the other buildings, this one smelled clean. It may
have been Roscoe's influence or simply a few bucks extra
to the super, but there were no garbage cans, cartons or
carriages in the hallway and nobody had swiped the hun-
dred-watt bulb that hung overhead.

But it was still a tenement and it was still on The Street
and for a second it hit me what a bunch of sentimental fools
the whole bunch were. Bennett . . . the old club, his apartment a replica of the original place, Wilse Batten in modern
quarters but still doing business on the old turf and Augie
waiting around to inherit, Benny Mattick and Dixie stamp-
ing around as barons and on top of it all the ballot box boys
at the call of the K.O. troupe. And off by himself, Roscoe
Tate, taking it all down for his sheet, racking their system
when he could right from their own ball park. Sentimental
slob or not, at least he was the only smart one. He didn't
have to take any funny money or any crap from the angle
boys and he had his fair share of loot and the kind of
prestige that counted.

Roscoe lived on the ground floor and answered my knock
himself. When he saw who it was he eyed me speculatively
a moment, nodded and stepped back so I could come in.

Sentimentality didn't exist inside at all. Roscoe had had
enough slobbery in his earlier days not to want to prolong
it in any way later. A studied hand had chosen the colors
and the pieces and in every way his apartment reflected the
touch of the bachelor and money well spent.

I said, "Nice place."

"I like it."

"That figures. You go it alone?"

"Most of the time."

"Well, you never were the one to waste money on a broad."

His shrug had a degree of contempt in it. "I still don't. They're free for me now like they used to be for you."

"Good for you, kid," I told him. His eyes flicked to mine a second, watched me with disgust, then softened to their normal ice quality and he waved to a chair and sat down himself.

"You didn't come to talk girls, did you?" Tate asked me. I shook my head. "Murder."

"So?"

"Have you been working close to the fuzz?"

"The police are happy to get anything I give them. They reciprocate in kind. Whatever's known about Bennett's death, I know."

"Don't feel so big. I have an ear at the big door myself. What I hear is that the cops think Bennett was killed where he lay . . . inside his apartment. Now, is this the latest or is this a blind?"

Automatically, his fingers plucked a pencil from his pocket and he reached for a lined yellow pad on the table in front of him. "What are you thinking of, Deep?" He was the inquisitive reporter suddenly.

"You give me one answer and I'll give you another."

His face had a shrewd expression and he nodded. "That's the only way they see it. Why?"

"Because that's not the way it happened."

"Go on."

"That small-caliber bullet didn't kill Bennett right away. He saw who hit him, got up and started after him. He lasted long enough to get to the alley between Glover's and Constantino's. You know where?"

"Sure, that's not far from Hymie's delicatessen, only now it's not Glover's and Constantino's. It's Mort's Dry Cleaning and Alverez the grocer."

"So okay, you know where I mean."

He made some marks on the paper. "It's an interesting thought."

"It sure is. It means the killer realized Bennett followed him and carried him all the way back to his apartment."

Tate shook his head. "That would be stupid. What difference would it make to the killer if he wasn't caught?"

"That, friend, is a catch question. I don't know."

"Then how do you know about the other bit."

"Because a girl put me on to something. You know Tally Lee?"

Tate nodded, waiting.

"She said she wanted to spit on my corpse like she did on Bennett's. It was a peculiar thought because she should never have had that opportunity to spit on Bennett. But she said it and she meant it. She wasn't kidding. Then an admirer of mine turned up with a souvenier . . . Bennett's watch. When he lay there dead a guy riffled his poke, lifted the watch and sold it. The kid who got it figured he was doing me a big one by bringing it around."

Roscoe Tate was excited now. His fingers wrote, although his eyes never left my face. His mouth was animated, seeming to mouth every word as I said it. When I finished he said, "Damn, you know what this means?"

"Sure. One of the night people could have been there to see who carried Bennett back. They're funny people, those. They live close to the shadows and see everything that goes on in every damn hole in the neighborhood. No matter where you go there's always one of them around. Eyes all over the place. You know, they used to scare me back in the old days. No matter what time it was I could always imagine someone peering out through dirty curtains or someone curled up in a pile of garbage watching what I was doing. Man, I kicked through more trash piles and knocked over ash cans looking for night people than I have hairs on my head. I found them, too. When I did me and Bennett kicked the crap out of them so bad they never remembered a thing or even wanted to. After a while with us they wouldn't watch. They'd just take off."

"You carry a mad a long time, Deep." He was grinning at me. The little jerk was happy to see me get worked up inside and I knew why.

I let my fists uncurl and grinned back at him. That much would make him sore and it was good enough for me.

He said, "Suppose I call this in," and reached for the phone.

I waved at him and he hesitated. "Knock it off. This'll keep a little while. The fuzz have their own stoolies. I'd like to stay a step ahead."

"Then why give me this?"

"Because you have your own sources, kid. They're not mine, but they're important. I'll trade you information as it comes. You keep me hot with whatever you get from your end or the fuzz."

He smiled and nodded. "It sounds good, Deep. Stick your neck out all you want. I'll be real glad to help you get yourself killed. Even to putting the stops on a good yarn."

"You and Irish Helen ought to get together. You have mutual interests."

For a moment he was quiet, then, "Don't do anything to

hurt her, Deep. You've always loused up everything and if you louse up her I'll do anything I can to hose you."

"Anything?"

"That's right."

I grunted and got up. "That's what she said too. Fine friends I got."

He didn't say anything. He sat there and watched me go out. But at least we had a trader pact and I knew Tate would come across. You couldn't ask for much more than that.

Bimmy's White Rose Tavern was a nothing joint that catered almost solely to neighborhood traffic. It had a local reputation for having great pig's knuckles and a good minor brand beer, and it was a rare time when trouble ever started along its bar. Bimmy saw to that. His three hundred pounds was a lot of meat to come up against. Bimmy wanted it quiet. It paid off that way. His back room was Benny Mattick's office and the long green that came his way depended on just how quiet he kept it.

I left Cat outside and Augie and I went in to the bar. We served ourselves at the glass knuckle barrel and when I threw a buck on the counter Bimmy came down to make change.

I said, "Benny in back?"

"Who?" His little eyes reached out for me.

"You play it cute, Bimmy and you'll get this knuckle rammed down your throat."

His finger slipped open the catch at the end of the bar and he raised the section and squeezed through. He still smiled the way he used to, his mouth pulling down at the corners, the scar under his chin widening with the grin.

Then he recognized Augie. Then me. The smile stayed

fixed, but he didn't move in at all. I said, "Be nice, Bimmy, and maybe I won't shoot up anybody in your joint. Especially maybe not you. Oke?"

He nodded.

"I asked you something."

"He's back there." I looked at him and waited, then his eyes shifted toward the closed doors at the end and he said, "Dixie and Lenny Sobel and some uptown gents are there too."

"Thanks."

We walked back and Augie played his part right and opened the door for me. He opened it fast and all the way so I was able to cover the room quickly with one look and spot the only two boys who were in any kind of a position to make a play. The pitch hit them too suddenly and they didn't move and it was all mine. I stepped inside and Augie closed the door gently, leaning against it as if he had all the time in the world.

Dixie lay on the couch, his mouth and jaw strangely out of shape. His eyes saw me, but he didn't move. Benny's mouth was still swollen, hatred twisting it into a painful grimace. Behind Lenny Sobel Harold and Al stayed close together, only this time Al kept one hand in his pocket. The other three who turned around were uptown all right. Uptown and on the fashionable side where the doorman saluted and pedigree was stamped on the doorbell nameplates.

I said, "Everybody's hurting around here today."

"Be smart, Deep," Benny told me. "What d'ya want?"

"Nothing, friend. I got it all. It's what you want." I looked at the three gentlemen from uptown and their faces flushed.

"Go ahead, Deep." Benny's voice was raspy, his bloated lips softening the Red Hook accent.

"What made you think you could take over, friend?"

"Who else was . . ."

"You didn't wait very long."

"The organization wasn't gonna come apart because you wasn't handy, Deep. You . . ."

I interrupted again. "I don't suppose you talked to Batten, did you?"

"So what's he got? You don't show, he got . . ."

"Maybe a million in enterprises, Benny-boy. But that's not big time when you can walk out with the rest of the package, is it?"

For a short space it was still. One of the uptown boys sucked wetly on a cigar and coughed out blue smoke. None of them wanted to watch me at all. They were on the wrong end of the stick this time, drawn there by necessity, but there just the same, the chagrin of it drenched and basted with the stink of hypocrisy.

Lenny Sobel leaned back in his chair, a lifetime of experience in these matters showing in his face as he weighed and divided the possibilities and at last, arriving at a conclusion, he said to me alone, "Do you have anything to control . . . or to sell?"

My grin was as nasty as I could make it. "I could have."

"But you don't," he smiled, then the smile went mean. "You haven't figured it out all the way yet and *you don't have it.*" When I didn't answer he said, "You've run the prettiest bluff I've ever seen," and with a barely perceptible movement of his head he said over his shoulder, "Get him."

I hit Harold in the hip with one that shattered his pelvis and caught Al in the biceps before he could make a left-handed draw. For one unbelieving second the little hood looked at his ruined arm then let out a long sob and fainted.

When I cocked the .38 I grinned at Lenny and watched the color run out of his face. Right then he looked old. A beaten, terrified hood who had stuck around just one day too long and now he knew it. Words that he was trying to say wouldn't come out and he seemed to choke on his tongue. Benny was watching, fascinated, his eyes wide and filmy looking. The three from uptown who had never been so close to death hadn't time to have the horror of the moment register yet.

I said, "Stand up, Lenny."

He choked again and tried to run and stumbled over his gunbearers. While he was still on his knees I put a hot one across his rump and he let out a hoarse yell.

"Just like the old days," I said. "Right in the behind."

When I laughed one of the gents at the table went into a hysterical giggle and didn't stop until he was out of breath.

"You, Benny?" I asked.

He shook his head. "I pass. You're crazy."

"Could be. Dixie playing?"

"You hurt him bad, Deep. He's popping every hour."

"Clean this mess up. Then pass the word."

"Sure, Deep."

"Tell 'em to get in line. That whip is going to start cracking pretty quick."

"Sure, Deep."

"And any more meetings, you invite me in, buddy."

"No . . . you got it wrong, Deep. These are . . . friends."

"Friends?" I said. "Three big pillars of the church calling a stinking hood like you friend? Don't be so damn dumb, Benny. I know these guys and their business and if you want to go on trying to give me the business you're going to wind up with a tag on your toe."

"Gee, Deep . . ."

"Shut up. Just get in line. That means way back. You never were a big one in the old days. Don't try to get rough now, because you don't even have a little idea how rough it can really get."

They said nothing and watched me leave. At the bar I picked up my forty cents change that was still there and said to Bimmy, "My apologies, fat man. They asked for it."

He didn't answer.

I said, "No need to remind you that this is a family matter, is there?"

When he finished his clinical study of my face he shook his head. "Don't worry. I know what to do."

Outside Cat was pressed against the glass, his thin body tense and shivering. He kept rubbing his mouth with the back of his hand, looking nervously up and down the block. I answered him before he could ask it. "Relax. They just got chopped up a little bit."

"Who'd you hit?"

"Lenny and his two boys."

"You're bringing it on fast, Deep. Fast!"

"Not really, Cat. I'm just slowing down the action a bit."

"Okay, okay. Just let's get out of here so they can blow their mad. Any nabs come in, we're tagged quick."

I laughed and we waved down a cab and got in. At the nearest IRT kiosk I told Augie to get the breakdown on all of Bennett's enterprises, listing every employee he ever had or anybody he ever financed. We dropped him off, then rode up Amsterdam to 101st Street where Cat had a room, picked up some of his personal effects and went on to the apartment.

On the stoop I opened the door and handed him the keys. "Stay put until I call you. Lock up. I don't want anybody roaming around here."

"Where you going?"

"To see a doll, Cat."

"Look, you better let me tag along. You forgetting those boys in from Philly?"

"Lew James and Morrie Reeves," I said. "At the Westhampton under the names of Charlie and George Wagner."

"Yeah. And they got contacts here."

I laughed and opened the door back of me. "So have I, pal."

Late evening was turning into early night when I came out of Maury's hole-in-the-wall diner on the east side of Columbus Avenue. I walked down to 103rd Street, turned the corner and started east. And there was Mr. Sullivan, looking at me with that same look he had when he beat me to my back with a pair of cuffs so long ago.

He put a hand on my chest, the motion almost a friendly gesture to any stranger watching . . . unless he saw the stiffness in the fingers and noticed how the night stick stopped twirling.

"The trouble's getting bigger, boy."

"Oh?"

"It's only going to end one way."

"I know, Mr. Sullivan. It *has* to end only one way."

"Always the smart one," he said.

I nodded. "I have to be."

His eyes were like glass. "The talk is getting bigger and stronger. I don't like it."

"What do you figure on doing about it, old-timer?"

"It's my beat, boy. My beat. I've been here a long time.

I've seen all the big ones, all the tough ones come and go. One day they're here, the next day they're lying sprawled in the gutter. A couple of them I put there myself."

"You're over retirement age, aren't you, Mr. Sullivan?"

The red crept into his face slowly and his hand came away from my chest. "Don't ask for it, Deep."

"Sure, Mr. Sullivan," I said with a laugh. "I'll do like you say."

I walked around him and all the while I could feel his eyes poking holes through my back. They were two holes, very close together, smaller going in than coming out, the way a pair of steel-jacketed slugs makes them. I shook off the feeling and walked on up to Grogan's market, opened the door into pitch darkness, my hand going to my pocket for a book of matches.

I tore one out, struck it and held it up. But I was looking in the wrong direction. Whoever had cuddled in the doorway smashed something down across the back of my head and when I hit the floor with my face there wasn't any feeling left at all.

CHAPTER VIII ━━━━━━━━━━━━━

Unconsciousness was only a partial thing. All feeling was gone, but there was still the knowledge of what had happened. There were still sounds from outside, vehicle sounds and people sounds. There was knowledge that my mouth was open and the incredible sour dirt taste of floor filth was on my tongue. There were things stumbling over me, then the door opened and closed, smashing into my head in the motion. But at least it turned my mouth to one side.

Sensation flooded back on a tidal wave of pain. It ran up my legs and back, then centered in my neck at the base of the skull. I got to my knees, spat, and when I could, wiped my mouth with my sleeve. I spat again, stood up and felt the sticky wetness oozing down through my hair. It took a full minute of standing propped against the wall before I felt like moving and when I did my foot nudged the makeshift sap and it rolled across the floor. By the light of a match I could still see some of my hair stuck to the tacky side of the soda bottle and all I could think of was how lucky I had it when the thing didn't break and slice me open like a peeled banana.

When I walked outside the street traffic was normal and there wasn't anybody at all who seemed to have special eyes for the doorway. There was an old man looking in Grogan's window and I tapped him on the arm.

"You see anybody come out of here, mister?"

He turned, looked at me, then past me to the doorway. His shrug was a universal gesture of the neighborhood. "I see nobody."

I grunted, rubbed my hand across my head and let him see the blood on my fingers. "I just got cold cocked."

His mouth tightened into a grimace and he said harshly, "Them damn kids. Damn kids, all of them. All the time they do that. Stay in the vestibule with the light out and hit you when you come in. Every night I hear. You shouldn't go in without light being on. They killed old Julian Chaser like that. For thirty cents they got." He spat disgustedly and walked away, his advice given and his contempt of humanity more firm than ever.

Then I swore under my breath, reached for my pocket and felt the wallet still there and the rod in the belt rig. I swore again as I slammed the door open and ran up the stairs, stumbling over the junk piled around the landings.

The door was open, the inside dark. I felt for the light, snapped it on and stood there waiting, the gun heavy in my fist. I sidled across the room, groped for the light in the bedroom and pulled it. I was careless as hell and if another gun was there waiting for me I was going to be all the way dead.

But there wasn't any other gun. There was only Tally Lee lying there with her head smashed in, the blood on her face not yet coagulated. She wasn't sprawled in the attitude of death; she lay in the relaxed position of sleep and she was lucky. She never knew what hit her.

I knew what hit her, though. I had tasted of it downstairs earlier.

For a few seconds I just stood there and took in the details. There was only one out of place and that was the throw rug kicked to one side almost violently when there hadn't been but one violent act in the room.

One other detail was there and it was a couple of minutes before it made sense. When it did the throw rug made sense too and the back of my head began to pound again and I wanted to shoot somebody so bad I could taste it.

Beautiful Irish Helen's coat was hung on a rack in a corner of the room.

I called to her quietly but there was no answer. I called again and parted the drapes that separated the living room from the others. The street light coming in the uncurtained windows outlined the few pieces of furniture. I saw a floor lamp to one side, found the switch and turned it.

Every motion I made was instinctive. My mind was a numb thing that wanted to see or know nothing, shocked with the knowledge that Helen, who lay there sprawled half off the couch with a thin line of blood running down her cheek, was dead too.

My fingers found a pulse, then my mind came back alive again and I lifted her to the couch. The crazy mad inside me made my hands shake and pulled my body so tight that every movement was almost awkward.

There was a lump under her hair and the skin was broken, but it was no more than that. I wet a towel, wiped her face and waited until a soft moan moved her mouth.

"Helen . . . Helen."

She moved her head and her eyes squinted with agony. I held the towel against her and stroked her face until she opened her eyes. They were blank at first, then puzzled. I said, "What happened, honey?"

Memory of it returned slowly. I could see it come back, reaching for an answer. "Deep?"

I squeezed her face gently. "You're okay, baby?"

Plaintively she said, "Deep?"

"Easy, sugar. It's me."

Then it hit her all at once and her eyes were great big things alive with terror and before she could scream I put my hand over her mouth and held her head close to me.

When it passed I looked down at her. "What happened?"

Her tongue wet her lips. "The door . . . I answered the door. I thought it was . . . you." Her eyes were wide, staring at me.

"It wasn't me, baby."

"When I took the lock off . . . it flew open. I fell down . . . and then something . . ." she sucked in a breath jerkily, ". . . Deep, what happened?"

"You got slammed on the head, kid."

"But who . . ."

"I don't know. He got me too."

"Deep . . ." She reached up and touched my face. "What happened to . . . Tally?"

"She's dead, Helen."

"*No!*" She bit into her lower lip to hold back a cry, her eyes filling up. Then she could hold it no longer and let it all come out of her in huge, gasping sobs that racked her whole body and I held her tightly until it passed.

I wiped her face again and sat her upright, and when I knew she was thinking clearly again I said, "Now listen, kid. Can you remember anything about him at all?"

She shook her head. "Only . . . what I told you."

"You didn't see his face? How was he dressed?"

"No. It happened . . . too fast."

"Did he talk?"

"No. I . . . don't know. No, he didn't say anything."
She frowned at me and glanced around the room. "Did
you . . . bring me here?"

"Not me. *He* did," I told her. "He wanted Tally. He
dragged you in here and killed Tally."

A shudder ran through her body and she stiffened under
my hands. "But why, Deep . . . why?"

"I don't know yet. I'll find out though."

"What will we do?" Her voice caught in her throat.

"Call in the blues, kid. There's nothing else to do."

"But Tally . . ."

"She was important to somebody. Now she's dead. Look,
are you all right? Can I ask you things?"

"I'm . . . all right."

"Good. Now don't make any mistakes. We haven't much
time. Tell me what happened since you got back here."

She licked at her lips and brushed her hair back from her
face. Even though she was sitting on the ragged edge of
hysteria she managed to stay on top of it all the way. She
let the tautness ease out of her body, then she clasped her
hands in her lap and stared at the floor, thinking back.

"The doctor was here then. He said she was all right and
gave her something. A . . . sedative, I think. Mrs. Gleason
from next door . . . that's the one who stayed with her
. . . went back as long as I was here. I fed her when she
woke up and . . ."

"She say anything?"

"Nothing . . . special. She was still pretty sick. I gave her
another capsule the doctor left and sat with her a while."
She paused and squeezed her hands. "Deep . . ."

"Yeah?"

"She was scared. Even when she was asleep she was
scared. She tried to scream in her sleep and couldn't."

"Go on."

"She said your name. She said Bennett's name too, but yours was the first."

"Repeat it."

"It . . . wasn't coherent."

"Just tell me. Let me fill in the blank spaces."

"It was . . . about how she could fix everything. She kept saying she'd tell somebody and he'd do it, or he'd know what to do. Then she'd try to scream. She'd say your name, then Bennett's."

I studied it a minute, then shook my head. "It doesn't add yet."

"Deep . . . did she die . . . because of you?"

I covered her hands with my own, feeling my face go tight at the question. "I don't think so."

"Don't lie, Deep."

"I'd never lie to you, kitten."

"Did she then?"

"I don't think so. Not directly, anyway. Somehow I think she would have gotten it whether I was here or not."

"What will we do, Deep?"

"Like I said, call the cops."

"What will happen to you then?"

"I'm not scared of any cops, kid. You should know that."

"Then call them."

"Sure, kitten," I said. Her eyes were hard again, patiently waiting to see what would happen. I helped her up, took her out past what had been Tally into the kitchen, holding her so she couldn't see what was on the bed, then went to the phone.

The desk said a car would be right along and not to touch anything. I said sure and hung up the receiver. I went back to the bedroom and found the check I had pinned to Tally's pillow on the dresser. I tore it up and flushed the pieces down the toilet. It was something she couldn't use any more now.

Then I slid the .38 off my belt, shoved it down under a pile of slop in the garbage pail, hauled the dumbwaiter up, stuck the pail on it and sent it down again. Then I went into the living room with Irish and waited.

Sergeant Ken Hurd had been an uptown kid himself. His face had been chopped up long ago by knuckles and clubs and there was no way at all to tell what he was thinking. His eyes were a cold light blue totally devoid of expression, but somehow, behind it all, you could sense the terrible hate he had. There were only two kinds of people to him, those who broke the law and those who enforced it. The good didn't matter. Usually they were just stumbling blocks to catching the other kind. And those were the ones he hated with a fine, thriving hate.

He had a big rep, this one. You talked soft and walked quiet when he was there. When he asked you answered or he was likely to smile a little bit and that was the worse part because there was something implied in the smile that meant bleeding trouble then or later and he really didn't care which.

They let Hurd work where he wanted and he picked the hardest end of town. He liked The Street because he ran an operation without complaints because if you complained it would be worse for you the second time around. Ken Hurd was a deadly cop.

And now he was watching me.

He let me talk, took it all down, watched me some more with an air of patience as if he were waiting for something, then let Helen give her story. Just as she finished Mr. Sullivan came in with Augie and Cat and the worms started crawling around inside me.

Sullivan said, "Here they are, Sergeant."

Cat took one look at the body on the bed and sucked in his breath with a whistle. Hurd said, "Know her?" and Cat nodded.

"Talk up," Hurd said softly.

For a second Cat went as cold as he was, then shrugged and said, "Tally Lee. Good kid. I knew her all my life. What happened?"

Augie volunteered the same information himself, then stood there waiting.

On the other side of the bed the Medical Examiner finished his examination, snapped his bag shut and flipped the sheet up over the body.

Hurd said, "What does it look like?"

"No more than an hour ago. That soda bottle's the weapon, all right. We'll make it positive later, of course, but there's no doubt about it as far as I'm concerned." He nodded toward me then, "If it got him as well, and we'll know by the hair comparison tests, you'll have a time hanging it on him."

"You're sure he was out?" Hurd asked him.

In a typical manner the doctor fingered the welt on my head as he went by. "He was out, all right. Of course, in a case like this you can always try for a self-inflicted bruise."

"Thanks," I told him.

"No trouble," he smiled.

The plain-clothes man who had been given the bottle came in frowning, the bottle impaled on a wooden dowel rod. He was shaking his head and said, "No prints at all. Everything's messed up. It's possible there may be something under the blood stains, but we'll have to let the lab finish with that first."

"Okay," Hurd told him. "Pack it in." Then he turned to Mr. Sullivan and said, "What about these two?"

"They were in The Pelican bar. Lew Bucks said they had been there for three hours and Grady the waiter backed him up."

Without changing expression Augie said, "We can go then?"

Hurd's snaky eyes touched his, moved to Cat, then took in Helen and me. "You'll go. All of you can go." We knew what he meant, but to be sure he threw in, "with me."

"What for?" I asked him.

His smile was all for me now. "For fun, Deep. I got news of a little rumble down the block. Nobody seemed to have been hurt, but there were blood stains in the back room of Bimmy's Tavern and some slugs stuck in the wall. It seems like you three had been seen going in there just before it all happened."

"Oh?"

"So I think it'd all be nice if we went over to the Green House where we can make an issue out of it."

Cat went a little white around the mouth and his eyes narrowed. I knew what he was thinking, shook my head when he glanced at me with a look that said let it ride. Augie caught the exchange and said nothing.

They called the precinct station the "Green House." The name had come down from a generation ago and still stuck, but it was only this one precinct that had the name. It meant there was something special about this place and there was. To those on the street outside it was like the Bastille was to some and the Tower of London to others. It was a tough house in a tough place and things went on inside there that weren't pretty to think about and even worse to be a part of. Somebody once said they broke more murder cases out of that building than any six others like it in the city and you knew they weren't wrong.

At eight-thirty I was in the Green House again after a long time and when I looked around all I could think of was that the fixtures had been changed a little but the smell was still the same. It stank of cigars, wet clothes and man-sweat held fast in an atmosphere gray with cigarette smoke.

Outside in the reception room they left Helen, Cat and Augie to sit and think and wait. Cat was sweating, dragging hard on a smoke. Augie was his impeccable self, seemingly unworried, but nevertheless concerned. It was Helen who had acted strangely. She was one big bundle of fury well contained and if the slobs had any sense they would have cut her out of it in a hurry. Any fuzz with time in grade should have been able to spot an innocent bystander without too much trouble and to throw one like Helen in with a rat pack was plain asking for it. So hell, let Hurd get his tail eaten out later. He should know.

But Hurd wasn't the kind to care. He and the other three stood around watching me and I knew what the pitch was. I'd go out soft and somebody else would break without trouble.

I said, "You going to book me in?"

"In time maybe." Hurd took off his jacket and folded it, then laid it across the back of a chair. He was a big guy, all right, heavy across the shoulders and in the arms. The meanness stood out in the cords of his neck and danced in his eyes. The others just watched, hoping I'd try to break out. It was a pretty old story.

"You're being stupid," I said.

"Okay, clown, tell me how." He loosened his tie and cuffs and smiled at me.

"I'm not booked in," I said. "You have no statement going for you. On top, I'm clean."

"Someplace you're not so clean. Someplace you got to be on the books, Deep. That's what I'd like to know. Where? Where did you come from, Deep?"

"Drop dead," I said.

He caught me with one big meathook and launched me off my chair onto the floor and when I shook the tears out of my eyes I stood up, set the chair back and sat down.

"What do you think about that, Deep?"

This time I smiled. I shouldn't have felt like that, but I was getting that crawly feeling again like I was going to explode and like with him, when I smiled, it showed. It was big and plain and real and I said, "Do it one more time, Hurd, and all of you will have to go on me, but buddy, you'll go hard. If I don't make it here there will be another time and another place. Keep your hands off."

"Threats, Deep?"

"Just telling you, buddy."

"So tell some more. Like about the blood in Bimmy's place."

"Suppose he tells you. It's his joint."

"Bimmy is scared. He isn't talkative."

"Aren't they all."

Hurd tipped the light up so I got it in the face a little better. "We'll find somebody who saw who was in the back room."

"Go ahead. Then get a complaint signed by them."

"You seem to know how it works."

"I've been in these places before," I said.

"You're right. We even have a record of the times. Would you like to see the records?"

"The hell with 'em. Arrests aren't convictions."

"You're playing it too hard, Deep."

"Is there a better way?"

"I hear you carry a gun."

"You shook me down. Did I have one?"

"No, but I saw your belt out of shape like it happens when you wear a gun in a holster. Since when does a hood like you get so fancy as to wear it there?"

When I didn't answer a throaty voice from the back said, "The old story is he wore a cop's gun, Sergeant. He took it from a plainclothesman some of them downed."

Hurd played it cute. "Oh, that's right. I almost forgot. He's a cop fighter. Like he just told me about. Is that right, Deep?"

I shrugged. Let him sound off.

"But to get back . . . what about you? You after the guy who bumped your buddy?"

"He'd be nice to meet," I said.

"Maybe you know who he is."

"Not yet."

"Supposing you find out?"

"I'll be a good citizen. I'll call the police."

"You may not get the chance. We've picked up some more rumors that make you look like a bad bet. You aren't liked."

"I heard that too. I ought to call for police protection."

Hurd moved in close, smiling again. "You're a real wise guy, aren't you, Deep? You got a big mouth."

I saw it coming and rolled with it just enough. I came up off the floor with my right going out and caught Hurd in the nose and the blood went all over both of us. Before the others could get in he landed two in my stomach while he got two for himself in the kisser and for five seconds it was mine, all mine.

The sap across the back of my head made it his and when I kissed the cold stone floor of the room with the flat of my face there was a wild sound of noise in my ears. I was still face down when I came to and Hurd was sitting in the chair he had had me in with a doctor taking stitches in his face. Over by the door Wilson Batten was sounding like a lawyer, waving a paper around while the uniformed cop tried to talk him quiet.

I got up slowly, grinned at Hurd and turned it off when I looked at Batten. I said, "It damn well took you long enough to get here."

Hurd swore softly. I wiped the dirt off my face and walked over to him. "I called Batten before I called you, friend. I figured somebody would make a try for my skin."

"Shut up and get out of here."

"The other three go with me."

Batten said, "They're all right, Deep. They can leave. I'll have a paper on them in ten minutes otherwise."

The doctor finished with Hurd's mouth, gave him a prescription to fill that he crumpled up and tossed on the floor and picked up his tools. I let out a nasty laugh and said, "I told you not to play it tough, Hurd. Somebody has to take you."

"Out, punk. There'll be other times."

"Sure." I wiped my clothes off, found my hat on a chair by the door and nodded for Batten. He let me go ahead of him out to the desk and behind me Hurd stayed close.

Cat's eyes went wide when he saw Hurd's face. Augie, as usual, was impassive. But it was Helen who seemed to catch the whole thing in one swift glance. Intuitively, she knew what had happened and her emotions played hell with her promise. She was all the way on my side. Big, beautiful Irish Helen had proud eyes for me and a funny little grin that said, *Damn, man, let's go.*

Wilson Batten waited until we were on the sidewalk outside the Green House before he gave me a light-lipped, "You're absolutely nuts, Deep."

"Not me, Wilse."

"You don't tear into anybody like Hurd."

"You don't play tough with me, either. Somebody had to tell him."

"All right, but if he wanted to make something stick tonight he could damn well have done it. Instead he played it smart and let you run so he'd have more fun putting the heat on. Listen, Deep, Hurd isn't any beat cop. He's got his own special brand of hatred for guys like you and now you're on his list. That's almost like being dead."

"You were lucky, Deep," Cat said.

Augie broke into a smile for the first time. "Not him . . . us. We would have had our turn next."

"See what I saved you, Helen?"

Her hand touched my arm. "Thanks." Her eyes shadowed somewhat. "Did he hurt you?"

"Not me, kid."

"Hell," Cat said, "when this gets noised around about him bracing Hurd there won't be a punk in the neighborhood who'll step loud around us."

I felt Helen squeezing my arm again, a nervous, impatient motion. Her voice was soft when she said, "Deep . . . does it have to be like . . . this?"

"I can't think of any other way, kitten. Can you?"

She hesitated, then shook her head. "I guess not."

"It's an easy way of seeing me get knocked off, if you remember."

"I think I'd rather forget."

Batten stepped out in the gutter and waved toward the far end of the street trying to flag a taxi. "Then you'd better start forgetting by getting out of here."

Automatically, I felt my back pocket, then patted my coat. I said, "I left my wallet back there."

Batten stepped back on the curb. "I'll go get it."

I stopped him right there. "My pleasure," I said. "They don't bother me at all in there. Let me have my fun."

The desk sergeant frowned when I told him where my wallet probably was and sent a uniformed cop to go look for it. I half followed him down the hall and while he went the rest of the way I knocked on Hurd's door, opened it and stepped inside. He threw a couple aspirins down his throat, washed them down with a glass of water and sat back as if he had never seen me before and waited to see what I had to say. I walked to his desk, took the pen from its holder, wrote a number down on his desk pad and said, "Buddy, I don't want anybody on my back at all. In this town there are connections to be had and these I got, so do us both a big favor and call that number. But in case you're feeling salty about that rap in the teeth, I'll let you get that off your chest anytime."

His eyes went to the pad, went colder still and when they looked back at me were even a paler blue than before, a light, deadly blue that was almost hypnotic with hate.

"You're really trying for big time, aren't you?"

"Never start at the bottom. There's nothing like the catbird's seat."

"I'll remember," he said, his face blank.

I said, "How far are you going after Irish?'

Hurd scowled and stared at me.

"Helen Tate," I told him.

He leaned forward on the desk, his arms bulging under his shirt. He still hadn't relaxed and I could almost smell the anticipation he had of getting me alone. "You like her, Deep?"

"She's an okay broad as far as I know. She's not involved with anything."

Hurd's grin came back again, slow and mean. "Anybody fooling around with Lenny Sobel or Bennett is involved with everything."

"So they were kids together."

"They were more than that together. They were real clubby, big man. Bennett angeled a show for her twice."

"He got his loot back. They made plenty, I hear."

"How was he repaid . . . in cash? Now there's the rub. It might even be something to think about. Maybe all this time you've carried the big torch for that fluff and when you came back you had to knock your old buddy off to pick up the pieces with her. Interesting."

I nodded. "But unoriginal. You get no needle in me with ideas like that."

"At least it's a starting point." His grin showed the edges of his teeth. "Come back again and we'll talk some more," he told me. "In fact, I may get out an invitation anytime. I'm making you my pet project, Deep."

"You do that."

"I will," he agreed.

"Don't forget to call," I said, pointing to his notepad.

"I won't forget," he told me.

I left, picked up my wallet from the cop, said thanks and went back to where Wilse had whistled down a cab. We dropped him off first, left Cat and Augie at my new apartment and then I gave Tally Lee's address.

Helen tightened when I said it, her head swiveling around to look at me. "Why there?"

"To pick up my gun. I left it under a pile of garbage," I told her.

We covered another two blocks before she spoke again. Her voice had that strange new note once more that was hard to fathom.

"Deep . . ."

"What."

"Why don't you just leave it there."

"Leave what?"

A frown creased her forehead. "Leave that damn gun in the garbage where it belongs."

"You really want me to die fast, don't you?"

She held it back a moment, but that was all. Her eyes got wet and she bit into her lip, then turned her head away with a jerk. "Damn you," she said.

"Helen . . ."

She cut me off fast. "Forget I asked. Shoot somebody. Play it big like you always did. Just remember one thing, there will never be any excuse for you to shoot anybody. You kill a man and the police will kill you. If they don't a jury will."

I didn't let her see my grin. "Your sudden concern is touching," I said gently.

Helen sniffed, shook her head with annoyance and turned back to me. She was all beautiful again, big and beautiful with ebony hair and a rich, hungry mouth. She smiled and said, "You know now . . . it isn't so sudden, Deep. It's just that it's all come back after a long time."

I tasted her then, felt the lush warmth of her and held

her so tightly she moaned quietly through the kiss, becoming hungrier, searching and saying my name over and over again.

Evidently the cabbie was a romantic. He waited until we realized that we were there, smiling at us in the rear view mirror. I gave him a fin and said to keep the change and he smiled again and said something in Spanish that sounded like sage advice.

We were on the opposite side of the street from Tally Lee's place and except for the single patrolman in front of the building you wouldn't have known that anything at all had happened there. New York didn't concern itself with the dead very long.

While Helen went into the drugstore a half block down, I crossed over, went through the basement of the building where Shriner Moe held Little Augie off during prohibition, climbed the fence in the back and found the garbage pail still on the dumbwaiter. I wiped the gun clean, put it back where it belonged and rerouted through the garbage to where Helen waited.

The drugstore was as good a place as any to call the apartment and when Cat answered I said, "You know where Dixie would be holed up?"

"Probably at the Merced Hotel. You want me to find out?"

"Do that, then stay on his tail. Keep Augie at the apartment and call in to him until I make contact. You got that?"

"Solid, man."

"Okay, put Augie on."

The phone changed hands and he said, "Go ahead, Deep."

"Augie, did Batten give you all of Bennett's records?"

"What do you mean?"

"You know what I mean. Are you sure Batten handed over everything?"

Without hesitating he said, "You can never be sure of Batten, but I don't think he'd play cagey with you. Those records I gave you were pretty complete. Bennett was mighty legal and always scared to death he'd fall on an income tax charge or something, so what he had on paper couldn't be kicked around."

"That's still not what I mean."

"Maybe you'd better spell it out, Deep."

"Okay. Like you know who was back there in Bimmy's place. They were out of Bennett's class but still in his crowd. Like Hugh Peddle and the others. Bennett had a long rope."

It took a few seconds before he answered, then: "Deep, it's one of those things nobody talks about, you know?"

"Go on."

"Never take it away from him, Bennett was foxy. Suppose he had a private file on the big ones. It wouldn't have to be much at all, just enough to tag that person and break him."

"It could fit. It could be what they were hinting at."

"I've often thought about it," Augie said. "Bennett never talked though. He called and somebody jumped."

"Did Batten?"

"Hell, Deep, Bennett never messed with the little ones. Those he could buy. What he had would be a power package."

"It would fit behind the refrigerator?"

He grunted, remembering back. "Sure."

"Okay. Go through the apartment. Hit every place you can and see what you come up with. The fuzz shook it down and it's possible that the killer did too, but one thing is sure . . . nobody found anything or there would be a new top man calling signals. Cat and I will be calling in occasionally so stay close to the phones."

"Right. Will you need help?"

"Not this time."

"You bracing somebody?"

"In a manner of speaking. It won't take much."

"All right. I don't suppose I have to remind you about Lew James and Morrie Reeves. Cat is all shook at you traveling alone even if he doesn't mention it."

"I know the route, kid," I reminded him.

"Sure you do. Just keep it cool."

I told him I would and hung up.

Helen was watching me through the glass of the booth and when I pulled the door open she said, "You won't go alone, Deep."

I leaned over and kissed her. She was so big I didn't have to lean far at all and even with that brief touch I could feel the fire start again. "I never expected to, Irish," I said.

Hugh Peddle wasn't hard to find. His ready availability to any and all had brought him to the top politically and it was his own personal order that he was ready to see friend or enemy anytime. This time he was in Walter Lico's Blue Pheasant Inn just off Broadway in midtown Manhattan having a late supper with Benny-from-Brooklyn. Their table was nearly in the middle of the room, surrounded by dozens of others, all filled, and as safe a place to talk business as any. If the muscle boys were around they must have had their backs to me because I saw neither.

Without being asked I pulled an empty chair out for Helen, seated her and took the other.

Their reaction was beautifully casual and unimportant, nothing showing that might draw a curious eye from another table. An almost-friendly nod, a courteous finger wave to a waiter for a menu, a simple ordering of two more coffees and then Hugh Peddle said, "Are you prepared to take me up on my offer?"

Benny looked up slowly, but I had seen that look before and knew he wasn't in on the deal Hugh had offered me.

I said, "If I took it, it would be at twice the price."

He didn't hesitate. "Well?"

"I got something else to do first."

Benny reached over and tapped the back of my hand. "Deep, the next thing you got to do is drop dead. You're just not big enough to set up shop around here."

"You got a short memory, kid. You forgot already what happened in Bimmy's."

Benny's face turned wooden.

"I could do it right now all over again and if you don't think so, just keep talking like that."

He licked his lips without wetting them. "You're crazy," he said almost to himself.

The waiter came then, put down our coffee and left. I said, "Peddle . . . what did Bennett have on you?"

His drink stopped halfway to his mouth. "What are you getting at?"

"You know what I mean."

"Do I?"

"Let's say this, Bennett operated with a sharp eye. He knew who had potential and who didn't and the ones who showed promise he went after until he had something big over their heads and held it until it could be useful to him."

Peddle shrugged and said nothing. Benny Mattick glowered, hunching his shoulders under his jacket.

"What was it he had on you, Councilman?"

"I don't like guessing games."

"Let's not kid each other. I knew Bennett when. I knew him like a book, inside and out and he knew me the same way. Twenty-five years ago we laid out a plan of operation and that was the way it would be. It was a long-range plan that was damned adult thinking and Bennett stuck to every detail of it from that day on. We knew where we were going then."

Hugh Peddle smiled grimly and sipped his drink. "If you know so much, then you hold the cards." The grin became a chuckle. "But there are no cards, otherwise you'd show them."

I shook my head. "Not yet, Hugh. This game just started. The stakes aren't high enough yet. There's a lot of bidding to do."

His grin was a plain sneer now. He was thinking ahead and thought he had me. "I think you've cut into the wrong game, Deep. I can't figure you for a threat at all."

"No? Well somebody does. Enough to get a couple of imports to knock me off."

"So?" Hugh's face grimaced with pleasure, the fat creasing around his eyes. "It sounds like a good idea. You think it was my doing?"

"No," I said. "Not you. I don't think you'd bother when you have your own boys handy." I glanced over at Benny. "Now you take buddy Mattick there, he might think of it."

Benny jerked and looked about him almost wildly.

"But I don't think he did either. He knows what would happen. I'm no slob to leave myself uncovered. If they got me then Benny would be the first to go afterwards and he knows it. In fact, it would do Benny good to make sure I stay alive."

Hugh's eyes squinted and searched my face. He put down his drink and leaned across the table. "Tell me, Deep . . . where did you come from?"

"Far away from you, Councilman."

"What are you there?"

It seemed that the whole room was quiet when it really wasn't. Benny was looking at me and beside me, Helen was motionless, watching me, waiting.

I grinned. "Big."

"So big that if you get killed your troops'll come in shooting, is that it?"

Helen's hand on my arm tightened involuntarily. "That, friend," I said, "is exactly it. This is my own private pet project, but they're all standing by in case I get in a bind." I let out a sharp laugh as I watched his face. He knew it wasn't a bluff. He knew what I said would happen and he let it roll around in his mind until he had the pieces in place.

"You don't have gang wars any more, Deep."

"No?"

Hugh's mouth tightened into a lipless snarl. "Let me tell you something, Deep . . . you know what happened to Dutch Shultz? Sure you do. The mob hit him because he endangered their operation. If they hadn't, the cops would have gone all out to wipe out the mob. It's still like that, see? Maybe where you come from they don't play like that, but if you stick your neck out and get it chopped off there's going to be a lot of organizational work done on your bunch from both ends of the stick. Brother, you not *that* big. You don't take cops and . . ." he paused, reaching for the word, then, ". . . the rest without losing. Believe me, if you were that big, Deep, I would have heard about you. Everybody would have heard about you. You don't stay hidden and stay that big. Nobody does."

I let him finish, then added, "Let's say nobody *else*. Just me. I'm the exception."

It was my tone that stopped him. His eyes couldn't hold on my face any longer and to take the edge off he reached for his drink. Benny sat there with the cords in his neck showing, the hate so fierce inside him you could almost smell it.

"And you're wrong, Hugh. If I get hit, you'll fall. All the way. You'll take the big six-foot fall, you know what I mean?"

He finished his drink and signaled for another. When it

came, he tasted it, put it down and said, "You could be worse than Bennett."

"What did he have on you, Councilman?"

"Why, nothing. Nothing at all."

I laughed again, softly. "I'm going to find out, buddy. You see, Bennett didn't die for nothing. He was a threat. He had a lot of people by the throat and every one of them was the wrong kind to have. They couldn't move in because what he had was too big to buck, but one day he got to be too big of a threat and somebody took the chance anyway and knocked him off. Trouble was, whatever Bennett held over his head the killer didn't get and laying around someplace is a large package of trouble."

"You think so?" Peddle said noncommittally.

I nodded gravely and grinned. "I think so."

"But if you knew you'd have it now and be making a deal."

"Maybe. But I know this, Councilman. I'm going to find it."

"Oh?"

"That's right. You know why? Because nobody ever knew Bennett like I knew him. For me only he left a clue some-place . . . somewhere he'd be certain I'd come across it and could take up where he left off just like we said we'd do twenty-five years ago. Pretty soon now I'm going to re-member what that vital piece of information was and then I'll have it and you guys'll be sweating your piles out. Mean-time every one of you are going to stand pat. You're going to be hurting like crazy and the first one out of line gets shot a little bit. You heard what happened in Bimmy's so if you think I won't throw a slug into somebody you're nuts, pal, plain nuts."

Hugh's voice had gone hoarse. "What do you want from me?"

I stood up and pulled Helen's chair back. "Bennett's killer," I said. "Maybe you can help find him. You're the big political wheel with a finger in every pie. Thanks for the coffee."

When we walked away I could feel their eyes follow me. As we neared the door I saw Hugh's two gunbearers. They were watching me too, so I nodded politely and since we were more or less all in the same game and this wasn't the time or place for their special services, they nodded back knowing we both understood the situation like old pros and there were no hard feelings.

Before we left I called Augie. Cat had phoned in a few minutes earlier and said Dixie was in his room at the Merced and he'd stick with him until I got there. So far Augie hadn't come up with anything but was still looking. I told him to keep at it until we were sure the place was clean and stay there until I got in.

It was difficult to know what Helen was thinking. The disapproval of anything I did was well hidden; the concern I knew she felt didn't show at all. It was as if she were lost in the middle of some remote problem, studying it for a way out. She took my arm, held herself close to me and when I glanced at her, smiled. I squeezed her arm under mine, waved a taxi over and told him to take us to the Merced.

Dixie was a pale lump stretched out on the couch. His mouth was still a swollen mass and all that seemed alive were his eyes. He was in slacks and a T-shirt, his eyes red-rimmed and wild-looking, yet showing the wily cunning of a main-liner with a fresh hole. He lay there, his fingers working as if they were caressing the haft of a shiv and he divided each moment between Cat and me, thinking who he wanted to kill first.

I said, "You want to talk, Dixie?"

"Hop it."

"How would you like for me to throw a gag in your mouth and shackle you to a water pipe up here for three-four days? You think I won't, then button up. Whatever I want to know you'll tell me, maybe even tomorrow."

The sweat started on his lip and his mouth seemed to quiver with the thought.

"How often you shooting up now, kiddo? Every three hours?" I picked his arm up and looked at it. He was pincushioned all the way up on both arms to actual scarification and probably popped in his legs now. "Think you can take a twenty-four hour dry run?"

His head rolled on the cushion and he stared at me. "I don't know nothin'." His words came out almost muffled by his swollen mouth.

"Let's find out."

Dixie moved his bony shoulders in a shrug. "So go ahead, big man," he said. "Take over."

"Bennett," I said.

"What about him? You think I bumped him, you're nuts. The cops already worked me over good. They tried to nail me. Batten got me clear."

"Not with me he didn't."

Something in my voice got to Dixie. He jerked upright and swung his feet to the floor and glared at me. "You lookit, Deep, I . . ."

"Shut up, Dixie. You just answer me."

He wiped his mouth with the back of his hand and nodded.

"The night Bennett was killed you were down at the liquor store picking up a case of booze, right?"

"Scotch," he nodded.

"Why? Bennett wasn't a big drinker."

"He had a party coming on, that's why!"

"When?"

"How would I know? He didn't tell me that. He was all hopped up about something, that's all I know."

"Okay, so you went down and got the Scotch. Keep going."

Dixie glanced nervously from Cat to me and shook his head. He shrugged again and wiped at his mouth. "What's to tell? So he calls up and says to bring up a case of rye too."

"Which you did," I reminded him, "in time to find his body."

He coughed, then croaked, "I didn't bump him. I was there all the time! The guy in the store, he . . ."

"I know what he said. He covered it okay. Good alibi. He's a good citizen with nothing down on him. Votes regular, sits jury duty, attends P.T.A. So you're clean."

"Well what do ya want with me? Jeez, I didn't . . ."

"Buddy," I told him, "if it were you who hit Bennett I would've read the signs. So would everybody else."

His eyes were scared stiff now. He didn't see what I was driving at but knew something was coming and all he wanted was out.

I said, "How long were you in the liquor store, Dixie?"

He got it out without thinking first. "Hell, two hours. Sure, all that time! The guy can tell ya that? Hell, we watched TV and chewed it that long. I'm clean, Deep, you can't . . ."

"That's a long time to pick up two cases of liquor, kid. Ten minutes to the store either way, two hours there . . . that makes almost two and a half hours away from the house. A pretty long time to run an errand. Bennett didn't go for that kind of crap. When he said to do something he meant like *now*."

Dixie's lips were too dry to lick. "What you gettin' at?"

"Easy, kid. You could have been part of a setup. The word goes out to stay clear of Bennett's place during a certain time . . . or if you get clear to make a call to let somebody know . . . and then *blooie*, Bennett catches it and you're clean. Almost."

He didn't like that last word.

"The cops figure like that and tie it in and you'll be doing the turkey act downtown. Cold turkey. Think you could take it?"

"Deep . . . jeez! Look, you know I wouldn't . . . hell, Bennett and me, we was friends. You know, friends!" He was perched on the very edge of the bed shaking like a scared bird.

"Why'd you stay away so long, Dixie?"

He didn't try to lie out of it. He knew it wouldn't have gone over so he simply made a nervous gesture with his shoulders and looked back up at me.

"I needed a blast, that's why! You know Bennett. He wouldn't let nobody near him if they was carrying a package. I couldn't stash nothing in his place either. I tried it once and that damned dummy housekeeper found it and Bennett beat hell outa me for figuring I could pull it off. He kept me up there so long I was going nuts. I hadda blast, so when he told me to get down for the booze I took off. I didn't have no stuff up here and called in for it from the liquor store. That punky stiff who brought the stuff took all that time to get over there. I damned near died. That's why I had to sit and watch TV. The guy in the store thought I just had a cold and fed me hot lemonade and aspirin and wouldn't let me go outside until I felt better. Hell, I was all over sweat and running off and when that stiff waltzes in with the junk I could hardly hold it. I let off in the men's room, gave the hype and the other stuff back to the stiff and he took off. So I felt better and that jerk thought it was the lemonade and the aspirins. He closed up shop and even helped me back to the apartment."

Dixie's face twisted in a grimace, not knowing what I'd make of it. "That all?"

"Sure. The cops come, they shook me down, but by then I called Batten and we got squared away."

"With your record it's a wonder they didn't hold you over."

"I was lucky. Wilse got there fast. Some strings got pulled someplace maybe. It happened faster than I thought it would. I was pretty damned lucky."

"See if it holds."

"What do ya want, Deep? I told ya, I didn't have nothin' to do with it!"

"There's something that's been bothering me."

"Well, say it."

"When I came in the club it was you and Benny up there. He was reaching for the catbird seat. Where did you come in?"

The tension was too much for him. He took a deep breath, shuddered and flopped back on the couch. "I was backin' him," he said.

"He need it?"

"Benny don't take chances."

"So you and the shiv go along. It was like with you and Bennett."

"Why not?"

"How come Benny-from-Brooklyn wanted to manage?"

"He never told me nothin' and I didn't ask. With me it's for loot and nothin' else."

I glanced over my shoulder. "Cat?"

Cat shook his head. "That's the way I got it too, Deep."

"Benny ever say anything to you?"

Cat's grin was small and crooked. "Who's gonna tell me anything? I only went in to get outa the rain. If it wasn't that I carried the old brand the new bunch wouldn't let me in the cellar."

I stood up and grinned down at Dixie. His eyes watched me closely, his hopped-up mind trying to pin all the angles down. I said, "One more thing. I shot up a couple of the boys in Bimmy's. They went to a Doc. Who?"

Dixie didn't worry it out any. "Halpern. John Halpern. Got a drugstore on Amsterdam. He got run outa the union five years ago."

Cat said, "I know him. He handles all the hot stuff for the boys."

"Okay, Dixie, play it cool. Keep your mouth shut and if you get any big ideas I want to be the first to know."

"Who thinks?"

"You better start. I want to know who killed Bennett."

He moved his eyes again, swiped at his mouth and watched us blankly as we went out.

Downstairs Helen spoke for the first time, tiny lines of curiosity tugging at the corners of her eyes. "You ask funny questions, Deep."

"It's a funny business, Helen."

Cat said, "What now? It's almost twelve."

"Nothing we can do now," I told him. "Let's drop Helen off and hit it. You want to go uptown, Irish?"

"I'll take a cab."

"What about tomorrow?"

"In the morning I'll have to make arrangements to see that . . . Tally's taken care of." I felt her fingers tighten on my arm. Her face pressed against my shoulder suddenly. "The bastards. Oh, the dirty bastards!" she said softly.

"Don't sweat it, Helen. I'll find out who did it."

She shook the hair away from her face and looked at me. Her eyes were wet, her lower lip between her teeth. "Not you, Deep. Please don't find anybody."

Then her mouth was a hot thing again, crying unintelligibly against my lips, her hands cradling my face with a wild urgency. I held her a moment, then forced her away gently. "Go home," I said. "There's always tomorrow."

She smiled, nodded and said, "Tomorrow." She picked a folded letter from her pocketbook, jotted down a number on the corner of it, tore it off and handed it to me. "Call me," she said, her voice husky.

I whistled a cab over, opened the door for her and waved her off.

On the curb Cat chuckled, "You got yourself a big one, Deep. She's all gone over you."

I liked the idea.

"It gets more like the old days every minute, don't it?"

For a second I remembered some of those old days and shook my head. "I hope not. Come on, let's go down the corner and find another cab.

You get a feeling sometimes that things aren't just right. It's like little things crawling up your back and across your scalp. It happens when you get to be a real pro in the game and can read all the signs and smell all the smells. It's a little thing that seeps across space and barely touches you, if it does at all, but that peculiar sense you've developed from running the back alleys and rooftops and living past the slugs and razor-edged blades . . . it tells you that something is out of joint and you only have a small time to find out what it is.

Cat knew it too. He knew it the second he got out of the cab and I saw him go up on his toes and make both ends of the street with an unobtrusive glance. I paid the cabbie off, tipped him and when I put my change back I did it neatly so that when my hand came away it had the .38 in it.

We didn't need any signals at all. Long ago it had been a well practiced maneuver with Cat and me and the motions came naturally. He laid back and to the left, planning every move the second something broke, keeping a split between us so we couldn't be taken out by any one person. He knew I had the rod in my fist and didn't object when I went ahead.

I opened the door, walked in normally and knew on the first step inside what was coming. I yelled, "Watch it, Cat!" and dove for the floor as a red wink flashed from the door to the side and with a quiet snap a bullet slammed into the wall over my head.

The .38 in my hand bucked twice before the other silenced rod went off again. This time it went off into the floor and with a harsh choking sob a body followed it down.

It took a few seconds for the echoes of the gun to diminish. As the waves of sound receded I heard feet hammering inside, a window smashing open, and I yelled, "The back, Cat . . . there's one going for the back!"

I was taking a chance but I figured there wouldn't be more than two. I hopped over the body on the floor, crouched and ran inside and felt my way through the rooms, trying to recall the layout of furniture. I made it to the back and saw the gray opening of the window pale against the black of the night beyond it.

There was no way for Cat to cover the exit except by

going all the way around the corner and if he ran his lungs probably wouldn't hold up. I got through the window, jumped the eight feet to the pavement and waited until I had the layout straight. Someplace not too far off somebody kicked a can and rattled it across concrete.

I didn't wait then. I jumped the fence in back, landed in another yard spotted with crates and strange garbage forms, picked my way around it and reached the seven-foot fence at the other end. If the yards hadn't changed any there was an alley between Glover's and Constantino's only now it was Mort's Dry Cleaning and Alverez the Grocer. That opening to the street was where the other one was going and if he made it he had it all the way.

Damn.

I didn't know the details of the route any more. Garbage piles change in twenty-five years. People nailed up the boards we had deliberately loosened and rearranged the backyard puzzle until it was almost a maddening maze. But if the other guy didn't know it either the edge was the same. I went up and over three more, felt my clothes tear twice and the second time a nail ripped a gouge along my calf.

Then there was the last one and I saw the guy up ahead.

He wasn't running now. He was down in a squat, moving crablike but fast. His hand was out ahead of him, the gun like an elongated finger, pointing.

I came up slow, getting him between me and the yellow light from the street lamp at the end of the alley and in that sick glow I saw what had slowed him up.

Mr. Sullivan was coming up the alley at a half trot with his service gun out, his hand fumbling under his coat for his flashlight and in one second he was going to be dead.

I had time to holler, "Down, Sully!" and saw him go flat. The guy spun, snapped another silent shot at me and when

I rolled, still another. That was all the time he had. Mr. Sullivan fired once from a prone position and the guy held his crouch a moment longer, then slowly sat down.

He was like that, leaning back against an empty cardboard carton when I got there, the silenced gun still in his hand as though it were a part of him, a small hole in his forehead.

Down the alley Cat was silhouetted in the light. He came up to us slowly, sucking air in great gulps, and when he saw who was down, fell on his fanny in the dirt.

I said, "Nice shooting, Mr. Sullivan."

All around us lights were going on in the windows. Voices called back and forth and somebody yelled for somebody else to call the cops. Softly, Mr. Sullivan said, "Yeah, you do that." Then he looked up at me. "Thanks for the warning."

"Don't mention it."

"I suppose you'll have a good story going for this one."

"Real good, I was attacked. There's another one in the hallway of the building. How come you made it in the alley?"

"I saw your friend here yelling and pointing this way. I catch on fast."

"Okay, then leave him here with Cat and let's get back to the building." I looked at Cat and felt his face. "You feel all right?"

"I feel . . . lousy, but I'll live. Go on."

Sullivan said, "A squad car will be along. Tell them to come to the apartment."

"Sure, sure. And Deep . . ."

"What."

"Watch it."

"Don't worry. Let's go, Sully."

Sullivan tried hard, but he was a harness cop long on the

beat and speed had left him behind years ago. We went on a jog and turned the corner as the sirens whined up the street behind us. There were scurrying shadows that darted out ahead of us, running only because we ran or because they saw the blue and brass. Trouble was something they wanted no part of, neither see it, hear it nor feel it.

The door was still open, gaping inwards on darkness. Sullivan pushed me aside, went in with his flash in one hand and gun in the other, found the wall switch and threw it up.

Automatically, I hit for the wall as the light came on, not taking any chances.

Sullivan looked at me and I looked at him. The spot in the doorway where I had gunned down the other one was empty. There was a big splash of blood on the floor and finger streaks on the wall and more by the outside door and what happened was plain enough.

Number One had been hit too lightly. He made it out while I went after his partner.

I said, "Inside, Sullivan," and went through the doorway. Behind us a uniformed cop and a plainclothesman came in with a rush.

When I turned the light on we all stood there looking at the body on the floor. He had taken at least three shots in the head and a few more in the chest and any one of them would have been fatal. But pros don't take chances and go for broke when they hit somebody.

Sullivan said, "That's Augie."

From in back of him Sergeant Hurd said, "Things are looking up, aren't they?" His face had a blue bulge on one side of his mouth that gave him a partial sneer.

"Can it, Hurd," I told him.

"Still tough?"

"Always."

A cop came in with his arm through Cat's and brought him in the room. In the light Cat had a sickly pallor and his cheeks were sunken deep in his face, each ridge of bone sharply outlined. He looked at me, his lips pulled back over his teeth, holding back the pain in his chest, and nodded. I knew what he meant.

The M.E. didn't take long to get there. He was resigned, but pleasant about it. The fresh kills he didn't mind at all and unlike a lot of M.E.'s, wasn't afraid to give an immediate opinion. He went over Augie quickly, established the time of death definitely enough to satisfy Hurd, put it between an hour and a half and two hours ago and said he'd make it official with a p.m. in the morning.

I told Hurd to call Helen and Hugh Peddle and check the cabbie who brought us to the building. Hurd was a cop who liked to see things done right away. Before he finished talking to Peddle who he finally ran down in a midtown bistro, he had the cabbie in the foyer and got a statement from him too.

There wasn't much I could add. As far as I was concerned they were prowlers who thought maybe Bennett left some stuff around and Augie surprised them going through the place.

Hurd took it all down solemnly, told us not to leave town and let us clear out while the techs took over. Cat said we'd be at his address and headed for the doorway.

I started to follow him when Hurd said, "Deep . . ."

"Yeah?" I paused, watching him.

"I made that call."

"Good for you. I got plenty pull, hah?"

He waited a few seconds before answering, his face tight. Under his coat his shoulders twitched like he was ready to use his hands again.

"Walk softly, Deep," he said.

I nodded, turned and got out before any of the newspaper crowd could make the scene. For Cat's sake I took it easy, but it was still too fast for him. We had to stop three different times to let him get his breath back before we reached his building. He lived downstairs in the back of a squalid hovel hardly fit for a dog, a single room partitioned off from the rest of the cellar with a single overhead bulb, a couple of rickety chairs and a faded maroon couch.

"Home," he said, and half fell on the couch.

He tried a cigarette, hacked himself into a state of near unconsciousness, recovered and threw the butt down. "Damn things," he muttered.

"Cat . . ."

"I gotcha, Deep. The dead guy was Morrie Reeves."

"You know what happened, don't you?"

Cat nodded, opened his eyes and looked across at me. "They thought they was hitting you. They didn't expect him to be there. Then they waited for you." He laughed, the sound rattling deep in his throat. "You shook 'em when you went through that door. Boy, when them pros miss a hit they can't make it the second time around the same night, can they? Damn, they didn't like your kind of luck, that's why the other one ran when you got his partner."

"I didn't get him good enough."

Cat turned on his side so he could see me. "I was wondering about that, Deep."

"What?"

"Nobody shook you for your rod. You walked out clean. Then that stuff with Hurd about a call."

"So?"

"Hell, man, I've seen the big boys who can make one call and back off the cops. Even shake up a precinct if they want to. Back in the old days when we was kids the upstairs boys even ran city hall. So I know when a guy's big. Trouble is, them big guys fall sooner or later and I hate to see you take the tumble. Been a long time since I had a friend."

"Don't worry about it."

"Where you been all these years, Deep?"

I grinned at him and shook my head. "Some other time, kid."

"Okay, Deep." He sat up and patted the couch so that the dust flew out of it. "Let's open this up and sack out on it."

"I'll take the floor, buddy."

"Don't be so damn snobbish. You put in time on this before."

I squinted at him in the dull light.

Cat let out a laugh. "This is the original of the one in Bennett's place. It used to be in the cellar in the old K.O. days . . . the first piece of furniture we ever stole. You carried one end of it out the back of old Moe Schwartz's secondhand store."

Then I remembered it and laughed. "Open it up, you sentimental slob," I said. "You guys just can't break loose from the old days, can you?"

CHAPTER X

I woke up long before dawn ever touched the rooftops outside and lay there in the darkness thinking. I was completely awake, totally aware of where I was and what had happened, yet sometime during the fade-out of sleep a new thought had come to me with such immediate clarity that I woke up.

And now I couldn't recall it.

I closed my eyes and tried to bring the dream back. There were no images in the dream; more like a sudden revelation where the facts are laid out and explained. Something like a blackboard where a problem is laid out and long parobolic curves touched related factors.

After a little while I gave it up and turned on my side to try for a little more sleep. I thought it would never come and just as it seemed as though it did Cat was shaking me awake and the light overhead was an enemy that ought to be smashed.

I said, "Okay, okay, I'm up."

Cat shoved a folded copy of the paper at me and tapped the two-column spread in the corner. "Roscoe's laying it on you again. You should of spoken sharp to that boy."

I wiped the sleep out of my eyes and scanned his "Uptown Speaking." It was pure Roscoe Tate, well reported, nicely barbed and effectively aimed. In brief, violence and death hit the former Bennett empire again, this time directed at the new headman and unfortunately tagging a lesser one. Two men were dead, the police investigation seemed to be deliberately hampered and the town was ripe for more murders yet to come. Next on the list would probably be a "former partner of Bennett who inherited his crime empire and intended to run it to his own satisfaction."

I tore the column out, stuck it in my pants pocket and got dressed. Cat was all for taking Roscoe Tate down some, but I waved that away. Tate wasn't doing anything he hadn't done for twenty-five years. In fact, he was in a good spot to pick up leads and if he wanted to do a smear campaign on me he was welcome to it. In this business publicity like that made the suckers shake more and gave you a status edge when you wanted to deal with another arm of the organization.

Cat said, "Have it your own way. Don't muss him. Wait till you got a gun down your throat."

"How?"

"Them uptown guys. They haven't said much yet. They're waiting to see how this thing blows. If they think you got too big a bull on 'em they're going all the way to get you taken out."

"Somebody already tried, remember?"

"So what? They won't pay off on a contract until the hit is made. That means Lew James goes after you himself or finds another partner."

"Lew James won't be moving fast for a little while yet. He's the one we want to talk to."

That made Cat's eyes light up. "He shouldn't be too hard to find. Let me see what I can do. I'll go pick up Charlie Bizz. He's one guy with an ear in every joint in town and he ought to know something. From what I know about Lew

James it ain't goin' to take much to get him to talk. Little of the old cellar treatment will make him yell his damn top off and there ain't no *Fifth* to take with us. That sound okay?"

Scrawny little Cat living on gravy time and going all out again. Friends. I said, "You be careful, Cat."

"Ain't I always?"

"Not always. You threw in with me."

"I know which side is buttered," he grinned.

"Okay, give it a try, but if there's any tough stuff you let Charlie Bizz handle it or get me. Now suppose we get over to the Green House so buddy Hurd can get those statements."

He nodded, picked my hat from the nail in the wall and tossed it to me. "Wish I could figure you, Deep."

"Don't try."

"Hell, Hurd never gave anybody a break before. He hates your guts and now he really must be churning. You're making him eat crap and he don't take to it."

"Tough."

"He's waiting, Deep. You can call down all the protection you can get, but someday Hurd'll have you standing right over a job with that rod in your hand and no protection in the world'll keep you from catching one."

"Maybe."

Gently, Cat touched my shoulder. "Like you told me . . . suppose *you* be careful."

"Sure," I said, "Just tell me how."

"Start by leaving that rod here for a change. Don't ask for trouble."

I laughed, stripped off the piece, waited while he stashed it and shoved him out the door.

Roscoe Tate was standing outside the precinct station talkng to one of the plainclothesmen I had seen the night before. He nodded wordlessly, finished his conversation and walked over to us.

I said, "Morning, kid."

Without any preliminaries he answered, "You had to get Helen wrapped up in this pretty fast, didn't you?"

I shrugged it off. "Relax, little man, she's clean."

"Involvement with the police doesn't get anybody clean."

"She did me. She was my alibi."

"That's what I heard. When does she become your accomplice?"

"Ask her yourself," I grinned and winked over his shoulder.

Roscoe said something I didn't hear, turned and waited for Helen to pay the cabbie off. She came up smiling, made a kiss with that lovely mouth of hers and blew it to me.

"Ask me what?" she said.

The change that came over Roscoe when he saw her was a funny thing; you saw it in parents whose kids had gotten out of control and were too big to handle any more, and in older ball players who just couldn't beat the ball to first when it used to be such an easy thing to do. There was a touch of pathos in his expression first, then bewilderment and just as quickly there was only a subtle trace of deep concern for someone he loved very much.

"Helen . . ."

"Hello, Roscoe." She slipped her hand through his arm affectionately and gave him a fond squeeze. "Now what's all this about?"

"You know what it's all about," he told her. There was no malice in his voice, but he looked up at me meaningfully. "I want to talk to you."

"All right," Helen said pleasantly, "but hadn't we better

go inside first? We told Sergeant Hurd we'd be here at ten and it's almost that now. Afterwards we can have coffee and talk."

Roscoe made a wry motion with his mouth, nodded, then walked toward the building. Helen held out her hand to me, tightened on mine to say hello and we followed Tate inside.

Hugh Peddle, Benny and the cab driver had already been in, their statements taken, signed and filed. It didn't take long to get ours on record while Hurd stood by in a seemingly casual manner, nodding as we talked, mentally correlating the facts. A couple of times he touched his mouth as he looked at me, reminding both of us that time was time and a moment of it was reserved for a special kind of meeting between us.

When the paper work was done I said, "You get a make on the guy Sullivan shot?"

"This morning. A real killer type from Illinois. The police there figure him for at least a dozen hits in the area and there's a sneaky rumor out that he's an enforcer for the *pasta* boys. He's the kind somebody pays a lot of loot to for services rendered. You sure have some nice guys looking you up, buddy. A few slugs from his gun were in your pal Augie."

"I didn't see it in the paper."

"It just came in an hour ago."

"Morrie Reeves," I said.

Hurd looked at me coldly.

Cat bit his lips and made a motion with his head for us to get out of there. Helen said nothing, but caught Cat's sudden nervousness.

"You're getting cuter all the time," Hurd said. "You know this last night?"

"Let's say I wasn't sure last night."

"Maybe you know something else. There was another guy

on the party who pumped a few into Augie too. The one
who got away."

"Lew James," I grinned. "They were registered at the
Westhampton as the Wagner brothers." Before Hurd could
reply I said, "I'm trying to be cooperative, Sergeant. A man
in my position has some curious sources of information, but
if I get anything I'll be happy to share it with you."

He leaned back against the edge of the desk and placed
his hands flat on its top. "You really pile up snow ahead of
you, Deep. It's good to watch you operate. I learn a lot just
watching. I used to watch Bennett the same way. He was
pretty cute too and had big connections all the way up the
line. He was smart besides. He never left himself open where
he'd take the kind of fall most big guys take. No tax problems or anything like that. No, he stayed clean until he
finally got rapped by some punk kid and that was that."

Now it was my turn to get curious. "Punk kid?" I repeated.

"Yeah, your old buddy Bennett was killed by some punk
kid. The big shot of the decade who could make mobsters
and politicians jump got bumped by a punk kid. That's no
way for a big shot to go, is it?"

Hurd watched my face with a peculiar kind of fascina-
tion, like I was some sort of unusual specimen.

"It was a zip gun that got your pal, a common zip gun.
You ought to remember the kind, you made enough of them,
didn't you?" He stopped, remembering something, then said
sarcastically, "I almost forgot . . . you didn't use a zip. You
packed a rod you lifted from a cop, didn't you? Still wear it,
Deep?"

I shrugged, opened my coat back innocently and heard
Cat say in a whisper, "Jeez . . ."

"A zip, Deep. A single .22 from a zip gun. Ballistics even

could tell how it was made. A section of a car radio aeriel, a nail-point firing pin driven in by rubber band action . . . pretty damn effective."

"Science is wonderful," I said. "This can't be top secret information, can it?"

"You'll read all about it in the afternoon editions."

"Thanks."

"Don't mention it."

Cat said, "Come on, Deep," and tugged at my arm.

I put my hat on and opened the door for Helen but Cat beat her through. If he had had a tail it would have been as bushy as a Christmas tree. He motioned me aside and in a low tone told me he was going for Charlie Bizz, then to look for Lew James. I slipped him a C note to take care of expenses and told him to keep in touch through Wilson Batten and to meet me later at the apartment. In no case, though, was he to stick his neck out. Helen picked up Roscoe at the entrance and we all went down to Hymie's together. Roscoe didn't like it, but he had no choice. Besides, he had a reporter's big nose for news and anything he got from me could be used in my obituary notice.

Over the coffee Roscoe didn't pull any punches. He came flat out and said, "Helen, do you realize what you're getting into?"

"I think so. I'm not worried."

"But I am."

She reached over the table and patted his hand. "I'm not a little girl any more."

"You're letting this punk con you, Helen. You've always been a sucker for hard tales and hard guys."

"Ease off, Roscoe," I said.

His eyes bit into mine. "Why should I? It's nothing you don't know. You're no stranger to this street. Just think back.

In school she pals with the hard-luck kid of them all . . .
Betty Ann Lee."

"We were friends," Helen reminded him gently.

"Friends? A kid from a tramp family who had more arrests
as a juvenile than any other two around? She was whoring
at fifteen and she was a friend?"

"She couldn't help it, Roscoe. You know where the money
she made went to. That family of hers wasn't much. They
lived on what she brought in."

"Okay, ours wasn't much either," he said, "but we made
out. When I kicked the old man out we did fine. Nobody
had to go whoring around."

"She didn't have anybody else to do it for her," Helen
said.

"It didn't matter. She would have gone down anyway.
She wound up with Bennett until she took a dive off a roof.
A damned narcotic addict throwing herself around under
every guy she met and this is a friend?"

Something buzzed in the back of my mind then. I said,
"I heard it that Bennett didn't want anybody playing with
H in his back yard."

"Pious attitude, wasn't it?" Roscoe sneered. "Just like you
guys. When Betty Lee took the leap it shook hell out of
Bennett. He wanted no part of anything that could dirty up
his little house . . . nothing that meant a federal rap. In his
business the feds would go all out to make a connection
between him and anybody in the narcotics trade. They'd
harass him to death if they thought they had something. No,
Bennett was shrewd. He kept all the way away . . . after
the damage was done. Now Helen here can't lose the old
school ties and stays friendly with punks she should have
shaken off long ago."

Roscoe grimaced, his hands clenched tight with anger.

"Now you come along. The worst of the lot. Worse than Bennett or Sobel or anybody."

"Don't worry about it," I said.

His grimace twisted into a smile. "I'm not. All I have to do is sit back and wait. Your kind always winds up the same way. Dead."

"You hate pretty hard, Roscoe."

For a second he paused reflectively, then shook his head. "Not really. It's a luxury I can't afford. If I hate I can't be objective, and if I'm not objective I can't be a reporter. Let's say I'm cynical and slightly embittered. After years of this street and turning the worst of things inside out to see how they're made anybody would be bitter. But most of all you learn patience. There's a certain course that events take that simply can't be altered and if you can wait those events will reach a conclusion. It's like watching somebody on a trolley car. They twist and turn, go up this street and that, stop and start, but no matter what they think or do, that trolley is following immovable tracks and there is only one end it can reach.

"You're on a trolley, Deep. You got on when you were a kid. You picked your direction, paid your fare and now you're stuck with the ride. It's all downhill, the trolley's lost its brakes and at the end is a big steel bumper that wipes you right out of existence."

"Nice picture," I said.

"You're all on the same trolley car, Deep. Capone, Schultz, Nelson, Dillinger, Diamond, Bennett and you. With you the ride isn't over yet." He paused, smiled, and went on. "I don't mind watching you ride it, Deep. I can get your obit ready right now and file it away until the time comes because I know where that ride will end." He lost the smile then, his eyes became tight. "The sorry part is watching someone else take the ride with you. It's bad enough when they pay their own way like you and Bennett, but when they deliberately hook on for fun's sake it's a sheer waste."

Helen got his implication and shook her head. "I know what I'm doing. Please don't worry."

"You do, Helen? You really do? You knew what you were doing when you let Lenny Sobel go soft over you? A hoodlum a dozen years older than you. You knew it when Bennett hung you on his arm for a decoration every time he toured the hot spots?"

She nodded wordlessly.

"You know it now too, I suppose. You're sentimental all over again over this creep because you used to have a crush on him."

Helen glanced at me and smiled. "This is what happens when you have an older brother."

"Let him have his opinions. He's worked hard enough for them." I looked at Roscoe over the rim of my cup. "Your simile is nicely put but has a big flaw in it."

"Has it?"

I finished the coffee and threw a buck on the table to cover the bill.

"Very plainly."

"None that I can see, Deep. Suppose you point it out."

I stood up. "Coming, Irish?"

"Can we meet later? I have to pick up a script at the producer's office in twenty minutes. I'll be free this after-noon."

"I'll call you later then. See you too, Roscoe."

"Deep . . ."

"Now what?"

"The flaw in my simile."

I shrugged. "A guy could get off the trolley any place he wanted, couldn't he?"

Very pleasantly, Roscoe shook his head. "No, Deep, not you. You're committed all the way. You can't get off."

"Hell, it's my nickel," I told him. I winked at Helen, she made a kiss at me and I left.

The cop on duty at Bennett's apartment wouldn't have let me in, but Mr. Sullivan told him it was all right, the place was mine and he didn't argue the point.

I looked at Sullivan's baggy suit and said, "How come you're in plain clothes?"

"Off duty."

"Busman's holiday?"

"Something like that. I have an interest in you. I don't want it to lag, especially after last night."

"Nice of you."

"Don't mention it." He nodded toward the door. "Do I get invited in?"

"Be my guest."

In the room where Augie had died the chalk outlines of his body still marked the floor. There were a few burned-out flash bulbs in an ash tray and the place stank of cigar smoke. The blood by the door had dried brown and after scanning the yellow pages of the directory I found a janitorial service who would send somebody right over to clean up.

Sullivan was like a big dog, tagging behind me as I went through the place. On the second floor he ran his hand over an expensive piece of leather-and-oak and said, "First time I've been up here. Funny how a guy like Bennett should live."

"Everybody to his own taste."

"Hoods don't usually like being salted down in a neighborhood like this when they're loaded."

"Bennett was a funny guy."

"Very funny." He turned and stared at me. "You going to stay here too, Deep?"

"You mind?"

"Remember what I told you the other day? There's enough natural trouble on the block without bringing it in from outside. I always mind trouble. You ought to know. I belted you around often enough. There wasn't one of you punks from the K.O. Club I didn't brace at one time or another. You know something? All of them swore they'd get me. More guys were going to put a shiv in me, brain me or put a bullet in my head than I can remember. You too, Deep. I remember you crying like a baby with the blood running off your head and yelling you were going to take me apart with your bare hands. You remember that too?"

I laughed at him. "I was thinking of it last night when that guy was going to plug you."

"Thanks again," he said casually.

"Don't mention it. I was saving you for me."

Sullivan grunted with disgust and turned away to inspect the room. While he did I went around the rest of it alone. There were little things to indicate that Augie had thoroughly searched the place and from the signs he had gotten to the ground floor where he was hit without finding anything.

I took Sullivan up to the apartment, poked around up there and was pretty certain Bennett hadn't used the building to hide his personal effects. I kept getting a strange feeling, one I realized had puzzled me since I started on this. It was the same thing that had awakened me last night.

Somebody had said something, somebody had done something or I had my hand on something that could tie this whole thing together. I was reaching for it when Sullivan said, "This place is familiar. Everything but the wall to wall dirt and the old back room for your shag parties."

"You caught on faster than I did."

"I hauled you guys out of that place often enough." He stared around the room, his hands on his hips. "Like being back?"

"I'm not particular."

"It figures." He looked at me, the years of watching the world go by showing on him, and automatically he bunched himself like he was going to swing on me.

Before his reflexes could take over, I said, "Anything you particularly want to see?"

"Uh-uh. You're the only one I'm interested in."

"You going to tail me around?"

"Afraid it'll spoil your reputation?"

"Could be. I wouldn't want that to happen."

"Don't let it bother you. I'll just poke around myself, the big, friendly beat cop who takes his job to heart. I always liked kids if you recall, especially them and their club activities. That's why I enjoy roaming around on my off time. Now you take them Scorpions that hole up in the basement of Decker's place like you guys used to in your joint . . . now there's a fine bunch of lads. Top-notch sports. Today I heard some funny things coming from their turf. Strange things."

"Lay off, Sullivan," I said tightly.

His smile was just the way it was when he tore me up with his cuffs so long ago. Big, broad and mean. "Deep, I've been around here a long time. I take everything that happens here to heart. I'm part of this place and proud of it and don't you try crowding me."

I waved my thumb toward the door. "Have it your own way, only get off my premises."

Downstairs Sullivan stood talking to the uniformed cop at the door and watched me walk off.

The janitor of the building that housed the K.O. Club was an incipient wino who hadn't changed much since I had seen him last. He had been bald at forty, with rheumy eyes and a whiny voice and we had used him to pick up booze from the liquor store when we couldn't buy it ourselves for being underage. He got paid off with a jolt or two and slept on the old cot in the back room.

Now he was sixty-five, the skin of his head wrinkled, his eyes still a baleful red and his breath still that of a practiced rumdum. But old Henny Summers still knew what the score was and how the game was played and when I knocked on the door he took a quick look, swallowed hard and forced a smile.

" 'Lo, Mr. Deep."

"How's things, Henny?"

"All right, all right. Mr. Batten, he called and told me this was your place now. You gonna keep me on, Mr. Deep?"

"Why not?"

"No reason. I done pretty good here. Place always like Mr. Bennett wanted it. Clean up every week and get it ready for when he wanted a meeting."

"Good."

"You wanna go through the place, Mr. Deep?"

"Later maybe."

"Everything's pretty good. Kids break in sometimes and mess around a little bit. Broke a chair once and stole some glasses. Last week they broke the back door to the cellar. I fixed it shut. This time I nailed it. Yesterday a little kid

threw a bottle in here. Knocked a pane out in the window.
I kicked his behind for him, I did."

"He needed it. Look, Henny, you know this building
pretty well?"

His eyebrows went up as he puzzled that out. "Sure, Mr.
Deep. Ain't I been living here all this time?"

"Bennett spend much time here at all?"

"Mr. Bennett?" His brow creased and he shook his head.
"He come for the meetings. Sometimes he threw a party.
You know, beer and that stuff. He never liked the fancy
deals. More like the old days. The guys in the ward, they had
a bit of fun. Nice broads too. Once one of 'em come to me
and right there she . . ."

"He ever come here alone?"

"By himself?" Henny's mouth turned down. "What for?"

"Any reason'll do."

"He used to stop by to tell me when he was having a party.
Sometimes, I mean. Other times he'd call up or send somebody over. Couple times long while ago he came over with
a jug and we talked about the old days. Talked a lot about
you, Mr. Deep. How nobody never heard from you or
nothin'. Mr. Bennett, he figured you had yourself something
going and someday you'd march back in and you and him
could take up together again."

Henny gave a toothless laugh and waved me into the back.
"Wanna see the old place downstairs? Mr. Bennett, him and
me sat there when we talked. Knocked off the jug and really
talked. Come on."

He didn't have to show me the way. There wasn't an inch
of the place I didn't know and not an inch had been changed.
We went through the narrow vestibule and down the stairs
and when Henny flipped the switch there was the old place
where plans and broads had been made at the same time and

Carlos Stevens had knifed the skinny kid from the French Royals who was caught trying to raid our arsenal and where Teddy the Lunger and I had fought it out with icepicks and both picked up three punctures before I got him bad enough to end it.

It was a big square cement-walled room with powdery white frosting all over and mildew touching the furniture. Henny saw me eyeing the empty space at the end and said nervously, "Cat . . . he took out that old couch. Mr. Bennett let him. If you want, I can . . ."

"Forget it."

"The radio still works. Sometimes I listen to it. When Mr. Bennett was here them times with the jug we sat and listened. Only gets one or two stations."

I stepped down the rest of the way for a better look around. The smell of dust and damp became familiar again and it didn't seem like twenty-five years had passed since the last time I was in here. The same curtains still hung, shielding the alcove off where the cot was and the door on one side to the coal bin still hung on hinges that had nails through them for pins.

"Mr. Deep, I got a jug in there if you'd like a pull? Kind of like celebrating the old days, huh?"

"Later maybe." I turned back to the stairs. "Come on, let's blow."

Henny seemed almost disappointed by my attitude. "Mr. Bennett, he liked it down here."

"Well, I don't."

"Mr. Deep, what'll I do with all the stuff Mr. Bennett ordered?"

"What stuff?"

"Fifty cases of imported beer and all those cases of mixers.

The guy from National Distributing wanted to know where to deliver it."

"You got me. What was it for?"

Henny's shoulders came up in an exaggerated shrug. "Who tells me? Mr. Bennett was gonna throw a party. He told me to get the big room ready for a big time. I ast him about the jugs and he said he'd take care of that end hisself. You know Mr. Bennett . . . he wouldn't let no jugs lay around here. He always brought it all up hisself."

"When did this happen?"

"Same day he got killed. You think I ought tell 'em to take it back? Don't suppose there'll be any party now. Hell, I didn't know what kinda party it was supposed to be anyway. Big stag blowout Mr. Bennett said. He was throwing hisself a stag party oney I don't know why. Just said he had a big surprise for everybody."

"Well, there won't be any party now. Tell National to cancel it."

"Okay, Mr. Deep."

I took a quick tour through the building with Henny in my wake, whining an opinion about almost everything and hopefully trying to find out if I was going to keep him on. When I said I would he quit whining and followed me quietly.

When we were downstairs again I asked him, "Did Bennett have a safe in the building?"

"Safe? No, sir. Any papers like after a meeting he took out. He never kept nothin' here."

The assumption was logical enough. Anybody could get into the building without any trouble including the kids. If Bennett kept anything big on board old Henny certainly couldn't stop them from tearing the place apart piece by piece to find it. Even if anybody thought there was something hidden on the premises they could always put a torch to the place and that would be that.

No, if Bennett had a package someplace it would be safe from fire, theft or anything else.

The only annoying thing about it was the knowledge that he would have made sure there was some way I'd know how to find it.

It'll be just you and me, Bennett, I had said. *Why the hell whack this town in half when it's only big enough for one of us? We ain't always gonna be kids, by damn. We shot out Sobel's behind. Pretty soon we'll be talkin' loud enough for everybody to hear.*

Damn right, Deep, Bennett told me. *These days you gotta look ahead. You gotta think big. Them other punks upstairs, they talk big but they all work for some other punk. Me, you, we're gonna be top punks. Hell, not punks. Big shots. Just like that. I can smell it comin'.*

And nobody could think bigger than me. *Sure. So why compete? There's other cities and other places. We stay here and pretty soon we're bumping heads. That good? Hell, no. So we split. We flip a coin and loser takes off and finds a new place to take over. That's thinking sensible, pal. No blood being spilled in the family for us.*

It wasn't new talk. We had planned it months ago and we knew every detail of it. *Whoever goes, Deep, I'm sure gonna miss you. Remember how we said . . . like if anything happens to the other one, his buddy will get everything? Whatever I get if anything happens to me you can have and you'll know where it'll be. I'll never change. K.O.'s ain't like them other clubs. We signed it in blood.*

Damn right, Bennett!

Okay, who'll flip the coin?

Wake up that wino Henny back there. Let him do it.

He woke up Henny who tossed the coin. It came up tails. I lost. We shook hands solemnly and I walked out to find my own turf. I had never come back until now.

Absently, I said, "Henny, do you remember flipping the coin?"

Henny looked back just as absently. He didn't even know what I was talking about. I gave him a fin for his trouble and stood on the street corner until a cab came by and gave him Batten's address.

A new Picasso had been added to the Gauguins on the wall. It was a smear of color and crooked forms and the signs of being expensive. Batten sat tilted back in his chair looking at it and when he turned his head the girl behind me said without apology, "He wouldn't let me call, Mr. Batten."

Wilse nodded, the girl smiled at me and closed the door.

"Don't spend money you haven't got yet, Batty."

"I can wait." He rolled over to the desk and made himself comfortable. When I sat down he asked, "What's on your mind?"

"Bennett."

"Ah, yes."

"Did he have a safe deposit box anywhere?"

Batten let a sardonic smile twist the edges of his mouth. "Still looking, Deep?"

"You got to dig to find gold."

"You find lead the same way."

"Don't be so damned enigmatic, friend."

The smile came loose and his eyes narrowed. "I didn't mean to be. I thought a blunt person like you would understand."

"It came through. Now let's speak plainly."

He waved vaguely.

"Did Bennett ever hint to you what he was holding over everybody's head?"

"Never."

"You were his only legal advisor?"

"The only one."

"You were aware, of course, how Bennett operated."

The chair came forward and Batten leaned into his desk. "Let's not be so specific. It was a conclusion I came to that was the basis of long examination. I see you came to the same one yourself."

"It wasn't hard. It was hinted at pretty strongly."

"Well, it isn't spoken of as general conversation, let's say. When you discuss certain people it's always quietly and in private and even then you can't be sure who's listening in. The best thing to do is keep quiet about it."

"I'm not the quiet type."

"You can be a dead type."

"But not until your connection has been definitely established."

"Like how, Batten?"

"If you're no threat you go out for talking too loudly. If you are a threat you get the ax taken away and get hit for trying to move in and wave it."

"Tell me about Bennett."

Batten nodded sagely, paused, then: "Unless you knew him well you would never realize that he was retarded."

"Retarded!" The word exploded out of me.

"That's right, retarded. He had more of a juvenile outlook on things than an adult one. You've been in his apartment. You know how he hung on to the past. Look at how he set things up for you if you came back. Your erstwhile friend was retarded."

I said, "He did pretty well for a backward child."

"No doubt about it. Like all juveniles he had a shrewdness an adult can hardly duplicate. He had a child's callousness and a solid criminal bent that helped him right along. These are the attributes that put Bennett on top. He worked things from a wild angle that nobody but a juvenile would even consider and because he did he caught certain persons off guard and before they could recover Bennett had the ball."

"That doesn't sound like a retarded action."

"It isn't. I said he had a criminal bent. Bennett wasn't a retarded *juvenile* . . . he was a retarded adult. Along certain lines he still thought like an adult. A criminal adult. That, Deep, is a rough, unpolished, but accurate picture of Mr. Bennett as I see it. You should see it too."

"For me it's harder," I told him. "I only knew him as a juvenile."

"You were lucky."

I pulled a chair over and perched on the arm of it. "So Bennett picked up choice bits and pieces of people and held them over their heads. Now, the big question, where did he keep them?"

Batten sat back and stared at the ceiling. "I wish I knew. I really do."

"What would you do with it?"

Only his eyes moved back to me. "Simple. I'd make a lot of friends. I'd make a present of those choice bits and pieces as you call them to the parties concerned and sit back and enjoy their largesse. All legal, no trouble, everybody saying thank you and I would need no more."

Before I could answer the phone rang. Batten picked it up, frowned and handed it to me. It was Cat on the other end and he told me he still hadn't run Lew James down but hadn't checked out all the places he could be either. He had gotten to the Westhampton after the cops and made out a little better than they had. With the aid of a double sawbuck the desk clerk, who was an inveterate cop hater, thought he could remember a number that one of them had called. He couldn't recall it then, but knew it would come back to him after a while because it had a certain rhyme to it. Meanwhile Charlie Bizz was hitting the medicos a guy could see without worrying about gunshot wound reports.

Wilson Batten was waiting for me to clue him in but I didn't bother. When I put the phone up I said, "Supposing you figure out where Bennett put the stuff before I do, Batten?"

He meant it when he answered, "Then I'll tell you all about it. You see, I figure you for a psychotic too, and like most psychotics, clever in certain fields. If I thought it out, then so would you and I'd rather not have you on my back with a gun than enjoy the profits such a discovery could bring me. Life, after all, is worth more than money."

"Keep it in mind, friend. You have it pegged exactly right except for the first part."

"About being psychotic?"

"Yes."

"Does the thought gnaw at you?"

"Not the slightest."

"Time will tell."

I nodded. "You have any immediate plans?"

"Nothing I can't cancel."

"Good. Then you hold down that chair. I might want you in a hurry."

"I'll be waiting," he said.

CHAPTER XI

I dug out the piece of paper Helen had written her number on and called from a drugstore down the street from Batten's office. Her place was an apartment hotel in the west seventies and she wanted me to come over as soon as I could. I told her to have something ready to eat and I'd be there in twenty minutes.

She was more beautiful than ever, standing there in the doorway waiting for me. A black velvet housecoat accentuated the panther-black of her hair, the thin scarlet beading matched the moist redness of her lips.

Big. Beautifully big. She stood with one leg partially thrust out and the velvet molded itself around the fullness of her thigh in a manner more sensual than nakedness itself. She needed no open neckline to highlight the grandeur of her breasts. Their eloquence was evident in their proud thrustings, having motion and life of their own under the rich texture of the gown.

"Do I pass?" she smiled.

When I grinned back she took my arm and pulled me inside.

"Didn't mean to stare," I said. "It's just that I got a fetish for big lovely broads. Besides, black intrigues me."

"It's supposed to. To intrigue you even further I might

suggest that I haven't got a damn thing on under it, either."

I tossed my hat on an end table and sat down. "Suggestions, suggestions, never any proof."

She stuck her tongue out at me, suddenly flipped open a button with the tip of her fingers and threw the housecoat open like a pair of great batwings. I had that one brief flash of an incredible combination of black and white sweeping through curves and planes into beautiful hollows and columns then just as quickly the batwings folded shut again. It was exactly like getting hit in the pit of the stomach when you weren't expecting it and left sucking air and wondering what happened.

I stood up feeling disjointed and said, "Damn it, Irish, don't ever do that again!" My voice came out rough on the edges and I could feel the dryness in my mouth.

She didn't back off. She took a step nearer, then her hands were on my face. "Why shouldn't I, Deep?"

Having a shaky feeling when a dame was close was a new sensation to me. There had been many women and many times. There were other big ones and other beautiful ones, but never one like this.

I didn't dare touch her. I couldn't take the chance. I wanted to push her away but I knew that if I touched her at all the moment would be too explosive and I couldn't afford the resulting emotion.

"Deep . . . ?"

"You said it once, kitten. I'm poison. Nobody knows it better than you."

"It doesn't have to be like that."

When I finally could breathe right I sucked my gut in and stepped back. "Something just occurred to me, Irish."

She knew what I meant. She seemed to retreat inside

herself for a second and when she turned her head away it was because her eyes were wet.

"You mean that once I would have given anything to see you killed?"

"That's what I mean."

"You think this is part of that wanting?"

"I don't know. You're an actress. I'm not a good critic. There are times when I don't know what to think."

Helen turned, looked at me and there was no guile in her at all. She smiled gently. "You're not fooling me at all, Deep. You know how I feel and I know how you feel. Shall I be direct?"

I nodded.

"I love you, Deep."

She said it quietly, with dignity, as though she had known about it and thought about it all her life. She stood there watching me, waiting patiently until I grinned at her because there was nothing I could say then because she knew it all anyhow.

"Does it always happen this way, Irish?"

"I don't know. It never happened to me before this."

"We'll have to talk about it some more," I said. "Later."

Her face clouded somewhat and she folded her arms across her chest. "Will there be a later, Deep?"

"Why?"

"You're out to kill. You know what will happen."

Once again I opened my coat. Like Hurd, her eyes went to my belt and when they came back to mine it was worth seeing. She came to me slowly, her hungry mouth reaching for mine, her arms possessive and demanding, the body warmth of her through the soft folds of her clothes. I could still taste her after she took her mouth away.

"There's a big chance for us yet, Deep. Can we make it?"

"We'll make it."

"There will be a later then?"

"A long time of it."

"Hungry?"

"For you."

"You came up here to eat," she said. "Remember?"

"You'll do for a starter."

She laughed deeply and impishly. "Later." She tipped her head back and kissed me again. "But not much later, darling."

There was a new domestic quality about that meal. Sitting opposite her, feeling her presence there like that, realizing that the unfulfilled desire we had for each other would not be a vain thing charged the room with a tingling, physical sensation.

We talked and laughed and remembered back to days long ago when things were worse and at the same time better. She asked me why I hadn't married and I told her I never had the time . . . or the right woman. I asked her an identical question and the answer was substantially the same.

Over coffee I said, "Tell me something, Helen . . . after all the time you've lived in this neighborhood, what made you come back?"

"How?"

"To be friends with a pig like Lenny Sobel."

She couldn't meet my eyes for a second. She got up, took the coffee pot from the stove and poured herself another cup. "I don't know how to tell you this."

"You don't have to if you don't want to, kid."

She put the pot back. "It's nothing like you're thinking."

"Look, Irish, I've never bothered to pry into your business and I won't start now. You don't know me and I don't know you. There's a twenty-five year gap in our lives and that,

kid, is quite a while. It was your life. The only part I'm
interested in is the future, so whatever you want to tell me
or not tell me is fine with me."

Helen smiled, her eyes crinkling with pleasure. "I like
you, Deep. But again, there was nothing like you're thinking."

I shrugged and sipped at the coffee.

A change drifted across her face then. She leaned back
vacantly, deep in thought, and when she was finished she
turned to me. "I don't want to sound silly to you," she said.

I waited.

"Crusades are funny things. You came here on one ready
to shoot down your friend's murderer. Roscoe has his, always
being the conscience of the city, afraid of nothing and going
all out to get rid of the things he hates most . . . slums,
poverty, crime . . . the things he has lived with. And me,
I had a crusade too."

"Had?"

"It seems a little unrealistic now," she said. "Betty Ann
Lee and I were friends like you and Bennett. It's hard to
imagine that girls can actually be that close, but we were.
Unfortunately, Betty Ann had problems she could solve only
one way and every day took her a little farther downhill.
I saw her hire herself out to every cheap punk in the area.
She was a damn pretty girl and in the beginning she was
exclusively for the big ones and Lenny Sobel had priority
rights there. From him she graduated down through the
ranks and reached Bennett."

I stopped her there. "Bennett was a big one."

"Not girl-wise. He couldn't make a chick with a stick.
Any girl he ever had he bought. No, he was big some ways,
but with women, nothing."

What she said tied in with Wilson Batten's observation.

To me it was hard to picture, but then I never knew Bennett as a man.

"Bennett always wanted Betty Ann. She would have nothing to do with him while there were the others, but when they were finished with her Bennett saw a way to get what he wanted. In Betty Ann's condition it wasn't too difficult to get her to try Heroin. She had been smoking pot for years and this was just something else. Bennett hooked her, he kept her tied to him like that until one day she walked up on the roof of a building and jumped."

"Rough."

Helen shook her head. "Not for her. Death was a relief. But for me . . . well, it hit me pretty hard. I wanted to . . . to get even, I guess. I wanted to do something that would get vermin like Sobel and Bennett and the rest off the backs of people like Betty Ann and Tally. For me it wasn't hard. I simply let Lenny Sobel . . . cultivate me and took advantage of his friendship to wield a big club when I had to."

"For instance," I prompted.

"Tenant evictions for one. There have been old friends about to get tossed out by some rent-gouging landlord and a word from Lenny would suddenly make them kind and generous. There were kids in trouble, too. Lenny could pull strings that would make a conniving pimp trying to operate around here run for his life."

"At least your crusade had a noble motive."

"That was only the beginning. Actually it was Bennett I really wanted. It was he who was responsible for Betty's death. At that time I thought Lenny Sobel was the big one and wanted him to do something about Bennett. I found out how wrong I was in a hurry. Lenny wasn't about to touch Bennett. Neither was anybody else. In polite, but firm language, Lenny told me to stay away from Bennett and I saw then who held the reins."

"And Sobel was soft on you all this time," I stated.

Woman-pride flicked across her face. "He was in love with me."

"It figures."

"He kept his ground though. He was satisfied with my company because he knew there was no more to be had." She stopped, frowned in concentration and leaned on the table, cupping her face in her hands. "Bennett, then, became a personal score. It was a simple thing to pick up old threads. I saw him intermittently at first, then later more often. He sent me presents, bought into the show and would drop anything if I wanted to see him."

"How'd he act?"

Helen frowned again, biting her lower lip. "Strictly on the up-and-up. Girl-on-a-pedestal thing. All this time I was trying to find out what it was that made him such a big man."

I asked her the big one. "Did you?"

"No. He dodged the issue nicely. It was going to be a waiting game. Then he died."

Softly, I said, "Who killed him, Helen?"

She seemed to stare right through me. "It could have been anyone. He called the turn on everything in this town. That low-down snake of a man directed whatever he wanted in any manner he wanted."

"Think harder."

"One of the faceless ones."

"Uptown?"

"Yes."

"I don't think so."

The frown grew deeper and more puzzled. I said, "I keep thinking of something I saw when I first got here . . . all the big boys . . . the Hugh Peddles, the uptown crowd, the gray-flannel representatives of the syndicates themselves."

"At the meeting?"

"That's right," I nodded. "They were all sitting there listening to Benny Mattick proclaim himself king. The power boys, the money crowd, the mob reps . . . all sat there and listened to half-ass Benny-from-Brooklyn take over the club and never said a thing."

"But Benny . . ."

"I know, a nothing," I told her, "but the other night he was at a conference with Hugh Peddle and although Hurd claims to be one of the common men he doesn't sit in on supper conferences with hoods like Benny."

"What are you getting at, Deep?"

"I think Benny let a very broad hint go out that he was the recipient of Bennett's personal power package that kept everybody in line."

"You think he killed Bennett?"

"Benny was too cheap a punk to bother holding in line by the blackmail route. Hell, Bennett could have intimidated him any which way. Remember, Benny was part of the old gang. He'd have nothing to lose by knocking off Bennett especially if he knew where the stuff Bennett held was hidden. Even if he didn't know, he was in a position to make a threat stick. Nobody dared call his bluff since there was a good possibility that he did have Bennett's ear as an old K.O. member and was his benefactor in case of death. Bennett's so-called will left me, his old buddy, cash, etc., but made no mention of any fact file. That could well have been left to somebody else.

"So Benny tried for the big one. He could have killed Bennett then made the grab. Unfortunately, I showed up. I was the only one who could call his bluff. When I did, that

left him with egg on his face. Now I'm beginning to see
how he could have arranged for a couple of boys to come in
to knock me off. Cute. Very, very cute."

The entire thought startled her. It was something she had
never figured on. "Then . . . you think . . . it was Benny
Mattick?"

"I don't know," I said, "let's go ask him."

Bracing Benny without a rod to back things up shouldn't
be too hard. As long as he didn't call the bluff.

Benny-from-Brooklyn had changed boroughs when he was
ten but he had never lost his accent. We gave him the tag
because we had two other Bennys in the club back then.
They both died when they wrecked a stolen car, but Benny-
from-Brooklyn stayed Benny-from-Brooklyn anyway.

Now he lived in a converted brownstone off Third
Avenue in a fringe area that was scheduled for demolition
within a few months. Six buildings from the east end of the
block had already been evacuated and two razed into a pile
of rubble. A bulldozer was shoving the brick and timbers
into separate piles and two men with jackhammers were
attacking a huge slab of concrete.

Like most bachelors, Benny had the ground-floor apartment. There were no names on the two other bells at all.
I rang Benny's, waited and rang again. I tried the other two
bells and had no luck there. When I went back outside I
looked at the windows upstairs and they were blank, curtain-
less. Either Benny had the place to himself or the others
evacuated ahead of the demolition.

Helen asked, "What shall we do now?"

"I won't waste the trip over, that's for sure."

She watched me open the foyer door in a good old-
fashioned way. I kicked the lock out and splintered the wood,

but I wasn't worrying about what anyone would say. Benny's front apartment door was on the right and in case the bell didn't work outside, I knocked on it with my fist.

Except for the muffled sounds of the construction crew down the block, the place was totally quiet. I didn't fool around here either. I didn't mess around with any gimmicks to open the lock when a kick in the right place with two hundred pounds behind it would be faster.

Helen watched me nervously. To her, what I did was a criminal invasion of privacy and as cold-blooded as stepping on a cat. The motions came to me naturally and she could tell that it was a practiced movement and when she looked at me she knew I was enjoying myself and put out a hand to stop me.

But the door was open and I went inside, my hand automatically feeling for the rod that wasn't there any more.

I saw Benny and shoved her at the second the gun blasted out of the darkness from the corner of the room. Helen smashed into the wall, covered by the corner of it, but there was nothing there for me. I dove flat, rolled, felt my hand close on a small table and I threw it without stopping. There were two more shots that tore into the floor where I was then I heard a scramble from the other room, the slam of a door closing and I got back on my feet.

It was too damn dark. My eyes hadn't adjusted to the light. They still had a yellow spot in the center from the flash of the gun. I groped my way across the room, found the door and got through. A window stood open looking out into the growing dusk. I took a chance of getting my head blown off and looked out.

I knew what I'd see. Emptiness. An open courtyard exiting into a dozen other buildings. The backyard jungle.

There was no use going after him. I went back in the

front room and found the light switch and threw it on. Helen was still crouched breathlessly against the wall. I gripped her hand, pulled her up, then she saw Benny Mattick.

Her eyes widened with the initial shock of seeing a dead man and her fingers bit into my wrist like talons.

She still couldn't believe it. "Is he . . ."

"Very much so." I stood over him, looking into those death-glazed eyes that were slitted open. There were two closely spaced holes in his chest right over the heart and he had died so quickly that little blood had spilled out and there was only a small stain on his shirt.

"Did you . . . see who it was?"

I turned around. Helen was trembling now, her hand at her mouth. I said, "No, I missed him."

"What will we do?" The shock was evident in the sound of her voice.

"Let me think a minute."

"The police . . ."

"No. Not yet. I need time. Damn it, we can't afford to get tied into another kill together!"

I thought back over the time element. Benny hadn't been dead but a few minutes, possibly shot just before we arrived. If the killer hadn't used a silencer the shots would have been muffled by the racket the demolition gang made down the street. At least the guy didn't have enough time in here to do much more than pump two slugs into Benny.

Without wasting time I went through the apartment hitting all the likely places Benny would have used to lay something away. Benny Mattick had never been overly imaginative and he wasn't smart enough to be devious. If he had hidden anything in that apartment I would have found it. There were two dusty Banker's Specials behind the phony fireplace and a Colt Cobra in an archaic shoulder holster lying on the catch bottom under the lower drawer of his dresser and three grand in hundred-dollar bills in a pocket of a suitcase.

But nothing like I was looking for. Nothing at all.

Helen had her back to the body, trying hard to keep herself in check. I said, "The place is clean."

She didn't understand what I meant.

I said, "Nobody tried to shake the place down. Whoever it was came here for one reason . . . to knock him off."

"Deep . . ." her hands were bloodless as they squeezed each other, "they'll think it was you."

"Relax. Nobody knows anything yet. This was a professional job, kid, and nobody's letting the cat out of the bag."

"Could somebody outside . . . have seen him? Or us?"

"People don't react to ordinary things. Besides, this block is half deserted. If we go out of here in a normal fashion chances are nobody will see us at all. Look, I have to make a phone call."

"Please . . . hurry. I don't want to be here with . . . that."

"Wait out in the vestibule. I'll only be a minute."

The phone was on a table beside a corner chair. I called Wilson Batten and asked him if Cat had called in. He said he had and gave me a number to call. When he hung up I found the directory, looked up Hymie's Delicatessen and asked for Roscoe to come to the phone.

"Yeah, Tate here."

"Deep, friend. I have a story for you."

"Don't do me any favors."

"You'll appreciate this one. Benny-from-Brooklyn has been killed. I'm at his place now."

Incredulously, he asked, "*You*, Deep?"

"Don't be an idiot. I found him this way."

Roscoe's excitement mounted. "It couldn't have happened to a nicer guy. They all fall sooner or later when you come around. Hurd'll be happy to hear about this. I don't suppose you called him?"

"No, and I wouldn't either if I were you. Irish is here with me and unless you want the heat on her you'll play this one real cool."

"You miserable bastard," he said.

"Save it."

"Okay, let's hear your suggestion. I know you have one."

"Natch. We need the body discovered. You can say you came to get a statement from Benny and found him this way. Don't worry, nobody will spot us. And you keep your big mouth shut."

Roscoe cut the connection without another word.

I wiped the phone clean, checked the floor where I had rolled and had shoved Helen, saw nothing that could possibly have identified us and went out to Helen.

The street was quiet now, the crew finished for the day. The first edge of darkness was folding in around the city and as though nothing at all had happened, Helen and I went down the steps, turned west to Third and walked six blocks before I flagged down a cab.

Helen couldn't stop shaking. She fought to control it but couldn't get the thought of Benny lying there dead and the guy shooting at us out of the darkness of the room out of her head. I tapped the cabbie, gave Helen's address to him and got back to the building.

Upstairs I made her take a couple of aspirins and lie down and told her to stay there until I called. I threw a blanket over her, kissed her lightly and ran my fingers through the black silk of her hair.

Half chokingly she said, "Please, Deep . . . don't do . . . anything."

"Don't worry, kid."

"No matter what you do . . . it can spoil things."

"I'll be careful."

Her hair tumbled about her face when she shook her head with easy desperation. "Do nothing at all. Please, Deep. We have so much now. Don't go spoil it for us. Don't ruin it all. We can get out of this place . . . if you'll only do nothing."

"Honey . . ."

She could read the expression on my face. "All you need is a gun in your hand and you'll use it. We'll both be finished then. You know that, don't you?"

There wasn't anything I could say.

She said, "You have something in mind, haven't you?"

"Yes. The whole thing's tied up in that damn K.O. Club."

"Can't you . . . leave it to the police."

Some things you can't explain to women. I didn't try now. I told her I'd call or come back when I had a few more answers and would know then how I'd handle the situation.

At least it satisfied her. She let go my hand reluctantly and turned her face into the pillow.

You can bring them up tough and hard and even keep them that way, but when they see dead eyes and bullet holes punched in a guy's chest the horror of it is always brand new. That is, if they're normal.

I called the number Cat had given Batten and the receiver was lifted after a partial ring. I asked, "Cat?"

Cat seemed to be half out of breath. "Jeez, Deep, where you been?"

"Pretty busy. Where are you calling from?"

"You know The Welshman's Bar?"

I said I did. It was a midblock spot on Lexington in the Forties.

"I been waiting, man. You want Lew James, you better get down here."

"Where'd you find him, Cat?" I sensed the edge in my voice now.

"Wasn't me. Charlie Bizz ran him down. You put a big hole through the muscle where the neck joins the shoulder and he had to get to a doc. Charlie Bizz got the word out and found out who. It was Anders. You remember Anders? Doc Anders. He's the one they tried to nail a narcotics rap on five years ago and couldn't make it stick."

"I know who you mean."

"Well, he was guilty, all right. He was strictly a syndicate man. So Lew James knew who to go to and you know what that means?"

"Yeah, a syndicate hit. It's big. Where is he now?"

"Right around the corner in a rooming house. Number two twenty-four. He came right from Doc Anders' place to here so it must be a joint Anders keeps handy for something like this. Bizz stayed behind him all the way and I took it up after we made contact. You get down here and we'll take the guy."

"Give me twenty minutes. And listen . . . things are popping fast. Benny Mattick has been knocked off."

"Benny?" He couldn't believe it. "Jeez, Deep, who . . ."

"It looks like mob action now. Benny couldn't make his bluff work when he tried to take over the club. It makes sense now, at least in some ways. Remember the meet in Bimmy's? You know who those boys were."

"Sure. Them's the big ones. Front men for the organization."

"Chances are Benny was trying to pull a power play. He still could have convinced them, then we came in. When Benny crapped out there he had it."

On the other end Cat let out a chuckle. "Can't say we don't go all the way. No more kid stuff. Right to the top. Jeez, Deep, when I think of all the times we scrounged apples off pushcarts . . . and now this." He laughed right out and rasped into a cough. When it subsided he said, "If I live through this it'll be somethin'."

"Lay off the butts and you'll make it. Now hang on, I'll be there as fast as I can. I won't even stop off to pick up my rod, so play it cool, understand?"

The bartender said yes, he saw the guy I described, all right. He kept coming in and going out, having a small beer each time and looking like he was waiting for somebody. But he had gone out ten minutes ago and hadn't come back yet.

I knew what had happened. Cat was keeping a running check on the rooming house to make sure it just wasn't a blind where Lew James might have switched to another track. I'd give him another five minutes anyway.

But even then he didn't show.

I could smell it again. The wrongness. Something got screwed up and you could feel it in the air. I threw a buck on the bar for the beer and didn't wait for any change. Two twenty-four he had said, a rooming house right around the corner.

Which corner, damn it!

South was closest and I tried that and there was no two twenty-four close by. I ran, retracing my steps, feeling the eyes of the curious follow me. I rounded the corner, followed the numbers down but I was on the wrong side of the street. Two twenty-four was directly across from me, a faceless house in a faceless neighborhood. There was a pale yellow glow coming from a front basement window and the vague outline of a woman reading a paper showed through the curtains. Upstairs was blacked out.

Nowhere could I see Cat. The only thing I could think of was that Lew James had left and Cat had followed him. But I had to be sure. I had to check. I took the six porch steps in one bound, stopped in the outside foyer and knew that inside something was going hot.

Cat's shoes were there by the door, side by side.

Then the shots tore the night apart and a man's scream was cut off in the middle.

I went through the door with no attempt at being quiet. I let out a hoarsely shouted, "*Cat!*" and from upstairs he answered, "Here, Deep!"

Something smashed against the wall above me and splintered. Glass shattered with an exploding sound and then there was a single shot as I reached the landing and dove into the darkness of the doorway in front of me.

He moaned softly from a few feet away. I said, "Cat?"

"Up on . . . the roof. Back way. Get . . . him, Deep."

I mouthed some wild kind of curse and rammed through the rooms. I caught a table across my thighs and threw it into kindling against a chair. My eyes were adjusted to what little light there was and I spotted the open door that led to the stairway. Most houses had only one staircase, but this had been renovated. I went up the last flight and paused in the doorway. Nobody was making a sucker of me on a rooftop. I peeled off my coat, threw it through and as I did a shot boomed out from one side and the coat was hit in midair.

That's all I gave him time for. I went out the kiosk, cut to the left and stopped where I was covered by a corner of the exit and listened.

Downstairs somebody was yelling his head off, but up here it was dead quiet. I slipped my shoes off and put them down, then circled behind the sloping back of the rooftop exit. The gravel bit into the soles of my feet like small knives but I was past feeling it.

I stayed in the deepest shadows and when I found the position I wanted, squatted down until my eyes were level with the dividers that separated the buildings. In the background the far lights of midtown Manhattan winked at me, rows and rows of lights unbroken in their pattern.

Then the pattern broke. Just the slightest motion blurred the lowest row of lights in the Lever Building and I grinned and followed the shadows to the divider, bellied across and got behind him. He couldn't afford to be too patient. Time was running out on him too. Those shots had been heard and he only had minutes to make his break in, but even then, minutes are enough.

I came up fast, but I wasn't any Cat. He heard me when I was ten feet away, gasped, swung and fired in the same motion and the slug crackled past my head and ricochetted off something behind me. He never had time for a second shot because I dove in under his gun hand and slammed him against the parapet with every bit of my weight and strength. I saw his gun go up and over to the street and heard him swear as he clawed at me with a crazy determination and for a second he almost broke away.

My foot kicked his legs out from under him and we came up at the same time. The guy was good. He didn't rush. He

let me come in, feinted and threw a fast right into my head.
I deliberately dropped my guard, started to bring back my
right for a roundhouse and he thought he had me. He
started a jab that would have taken my head off, only my
head wasn't there. It went over me and I came up with a
jolting uppercut that lifted him to his toes. I had the other
one ready, but he grappled, hung on, and laid his face almost against mine.

I knew him then. His right name was Artie Hull and he
was an enforcer for the syndicate and the pieces began
dropping into the right slots.

Before he could recover I shoved him away, cocked my
hand, but the tricky bastard brought his shoe down on my
foot, I went to my knees and without trying for the kill he
spun and ran for the parapet to jump the four-foot air shaft
to the other building.

Somebody had left an antenna wire stretched out right
by the edge. His foot caught it, he tumbled three stories
down too surprised to even scream.

I got my shoes back on, picked up my coat and climbed
back into it as I ran down the stairs. No sirens yet, but
they could come up quietly. This time I found a lamp and
snapped it on.

Cat looked up at me from the floor, smiling. "You . . .
get him?"

"He's dead. What happened?"

He nodded toward the doorway on the other side of the
room. I looked in, flicked the light on and off quickly. The
guy on the bed had a bandaged neck and two fresh holes
in his chest.

Cat didn't want me to touch him. He held his hands
across him and his breath came in burbling gasps. I said,
"I'll get a doctor, kid."

"No."

"Nuts, you'll be all right."

He stopped me with a feeble gesture. "I had it. Why fight it. You . . . scram, Deep."

"Tell me, what happened?"

"I was watching . . . saw this guy come right up . . . go inside. I knew . . . who he was. Mob boy. Torpedo."

"Artie Hull. I made him too."

"Syndicate . . . you know?"

I nodded.

He coughed, the pain of it racking his body. Flecks of blood spewed from his mouth; he choked, got it up and a steady trickle flowed down his chin. "Tried to . . . stop him only I ain't the same old . . . Cat." It hurt him to do it, but he grinned.

"Deep . . ."

"Here, kid."

"See clerk . . . Westhampton . . . Morrie called . . ."

"Don't talk, Cat. I get it."

Like a cold wind in the eaves, the sirens whined up the street. Cat heard it too. "Beat it, Deep. Roof . . . like old times. Scram."

"I hate to do it."

" 'S okay." He smiled once more. "I know. Real . . . blood brothers, us. Old Knight . . . Owls. K.O. Really wasn't so . . . much fun. Alla time trouble. Still . . . that way. Now no more trouble."

He did a funny little thing with his fingers I hadn't thought of for twenty-five years. He gave me the old K.O. high sign. I grinned and gave it back. "You sentimental jerk you," I said.

"Blow, joe."

We gripped hands once. It was enough. It was what he wanted.

The sirens were turning the corner and time had run out. I went back to the roof, falling into old-time patterns and thoughts and the run was as if I had never left the rooftops at all. It was like being a kid again.

When I came down I was a full block away and headed toward Cat's hole in the wall.

I wanted my gun back.

The Westhampton was a hotel for the nothing people. They came and went, sometimes stayed a while, sometimes even died there. It was an inexpensive and indifferent kind of hotel where you could find people who lived dangling from a thread. Struggling actors and out-of-town hopefuls used the place until their economy moved them down to the squalid flea bags or up to the next notch.

I pushed through the door and scanned the lobby quickly. Two young girls in trench coats talked too loudly about some show while they waited for the elevator and by the front windows an old man in a smock dusted the backs of the chairs. Behind the desk the clerk was sorting mail out, whistling aimlessly while a transistor radio chatted at his elbow.

He nodded carelessly when I reached him, finished with the mail and said, "Room?"

"Cat told me to see you."

He was one of the nothing people too. He had lived too long among them and taken on all their characteristics. Any expression that touched his face was unreal. Long ago he had discarded emotion for unconcern and now he just stood there playing the game.

"Cat?"

There were two ways of playing the game. I showed him the first way that generally everyone knew and laid a twenty-dollar bill on top of the counter. "That's right, Cat," I said.

He eyed the bill and I knew what he was thinking, but his face stayed impassive.

"Cat," he stated, as if he were trying to remember the name.

So I showed him the other way to play the game and let my coat come open deliberately so he could see the rod in the belt holster and when I grinned at him he knew the game was over. "My name is Deep," I said.

Deftly, his fingers snapped up the bill and tucked it away. His eyes swept the lobby behind me with a practiced glance and he fiddled with the card holder in front of him.

"Cat said you thought you could remember a number. The Wagner boys made it."

"Yes." He licked his dry lips. "But they . . ."

"Don't worry about them," I said coldly. "They're both dead."

He walked his eyes from the pad, up my front until he was drawn to my own. He had read a lot of faces in his time. He knew what kind of people were that kind who could stand behind a gun and use it, and now he was seeing it in me.

"I won't . . . get rapped for this, will I?"

"You never saw me in your life before if anybody asks."

"That Cat, I wish he didn't ask. You tell him . . ."

"He's dead too, buddy."

"Cripes!" he said softly.

"What number was it!"

"Two-oh-two-oh-two. It rhymed. Sort of like a song. That's how I remembered it."

"Good. You remember the exchange!"

He said no with a quick shake of his head. But it was enough. I left him, walked across the room to the row of empty pay phones, climbed in the booth and shut the door. I got my party on the second try, gave him the number and asked for a listing of all exchanges that carried the number and the names to go with them. He asked for my number, told me to wait and hung up.

From across the room the desk clerk watched me like a mouse peering out of a hole.

Ten minutes later the phone rang and when I answered my informant said, "Ready?" and when I said I was, began to rattle off numbers and names. I took them all down on the back of an envelope and when he reached the sixth one I said, "Hold it," told him thanks and cradled the phone. A little mistake in judgment had come home to roost.

I remembered what Cat had told me. Two killers had been given a contract to rub me out. Later somebody had gone even higher to delay the execution. The killers called their original employer for further orders and were told to go ahead. That call was the mistake.

They had called Hugh Peddle, the sixth name on the list.

CHAPTER XII

The old Dutch district had undergone a face change when they tore down the tenements ten years ago. They built a new housing development in the middle of it, moved the people back in and now they had a real, up-to-date tenement section. The people had never changed; they talked the same, they acted the same, they did the same. They voted as a bloc for whoever offered the most for their vote and cared little about what happened afterwards.

Hugh Peddle had bought their votes with no trouble at all. He was basically a machine politician, but lately had been pretty independent because he controlled a section big enough to be a critical factor in any election.

And the people loved him. He was a local Santa Claus who took care of his own even to living among them where he was right at hand to solve their immediate problems, which were his problems too. Hugh lived in a quiet corner apartment house that had, thirty years before, been a well thought of address. But times and conditions change and the block the building faced was scrubbed by a better section an eighth of a mile away and gradually blended into the rest of the environment and was accepted as part of the Dutch district.

The bartender thought Hugh owned the entire building.

He lived, with a valet and a part-time maid, in what could be called a penthouse apartment if such a thing were possible in the neighborhood and had a private elevator to an entrance on the street. Below, the tenants were people well respected . . . two families employed by Con Ed, a city fireman, the manager of the grocery chain on the north corner and a wild redheaded artist who did a syndicated comic strip that was actually a biography of his own life.

I had a few more beers, paid the tab and walked out. It was exactly ten o'clock. Overhead a high overcast threw back the diffused glow of the city lights and there was a smell of rain in the air. It was like the night we had that rumble with the Delrays and Bennett and Augie had stopped the action when they fired a round from the zips Augie had fashioned in school that past week.

What the hell, was I getting sentimental too?

And I had that feeling again as if I thought of something and just as fast forgot it. A key thought. Damn. I put it away and walked toward Hugh Peddle's building.

The lobby was small, walled with mirrors to make it seem larger. To one side a door with an EXIT sign above it led upstairs. Directly opposite the street doors was a self-service elevator.

I chose the stairway.

Each landing opened into a miniature foyer that had access to the elevator. The elevator itself was opened and empty at the final floor it served, but the stairway continued another flight. I followed it up, opened the door to a small flagstoned terrace that ran around the penthouse and eased it closed behind me.

This side of the penthouse was flanked by curtained French windows facing the south. A pair of them seemed to be the type that swung out but I wanted to go around the place before I tried an entry. There was a door on the north side that evidently led into the kitchen area and on the west a rather elaborate entrance that opened onto a mock patio that held three fancy wrought-iron, marble-topped tables and matching chairs.

From there I could see a dull glow of light inside that would come from a night light or a small table lamp. It was too early to assume Peddle was there and asleep. The only conclusion was that he had gone out and given the servants the night off too.

The French doors on the south side were the easiest to open. A knife blade forced the simple drop catch up and I opened the doors, stepped inside and pulled them closed behind me.

From what I could see there was no simplicity in Peddle's way of life. The neighborhood might be in that slow state of decay on the avenue below, but here there was no awareness of it. He was forced by political expediency to live where he made it, but he didn't have to live like the others. Some things still could be bought no matter where you were.

Luxury, for instance.

I eased by the grand piano, followed the sweep of the room to the archway and paused. The light came from a room to my right and when I stepped into the hallway I saw what it was, a small table lamp in the far corner. I let the .38 drop back in the holster and walked quietly toward the light.

It was a library of a sort. Two walls were shelved with books, a TV stood at one end and heavy overstuffed leather chairs threw bulky shadows into the dim reaches of the room. I circled it, not touching anything, then crossed to the other side.

A polished mahogany bar curved out from the wall there, in back of it a blue tinted mirror and twin rows of bottles and glasses. One empty glass still rested there and when I picked it up the ice in the bottom clinked.

I had the gun out ahead of me when I reached the bedroom. The door was open and I could half see the bed. Somebody was lying on top of it unmoving and I took a step inside, feeling for the switch. In the sudden glare of the light I felt my heart slam against my ribs and knew I had mousetrapped myself like a damn fool sucker because the guy on the bed was tied down tight with a gag in his mouth and the snout of a gun was in my back against my spine.

A voice said coldly, "Drop it," and I let the gun go.

The guy behind me prodded harder and I took two steps farther into the room.

"Turn around."

I did.

I said, "Hello, Tony," and the slack-faced killer who worked for the uptown crowd nodded distantly, not caring one way or another. There was another one, a few feet behind him and to his left and he had a small hammerless automatic in his hand and looked at me anxiously as though he hoped I was going to break in and run for it.

Then Lenny Sobel came in smiling, picked my gun off the floor, hefted it and put it in his pocket. He looked at me, his eyes deadly. "You carry a nice piece, Deep. That's the one you took off the cop, isn't it?"

"The same," I said. He could drop dead before I'd take his jazz. "You should remember it, Lenny. I shot you twice with it. Both times in the same place."

Tony let out a snicker but when Lenny glanced at him, cut it short. "I've been looking forward to this, Deep."

"I bet you have."

"Big mouth."

"Always," I told him.

Before Lenny could answer Tony said, "We better get outa here."

"I'll tell you when," Lenny scowled.

The little hood did a Cagney with his shoulders. "Like hell. You work for the same guys I do. They said make it snappy and we're making it snappy. We missed Peddle but we saved ourselves a trip and got this one so we're halfway home. Let's get back there."

Lenny didn't like to be reminded that he was under orders. His face was hard and black and every ounce of his hate was poured out at me. I wanted a bigger picture than I got so I made a motion toward the bed with the back of my head and said, "The butler'll talk, Lenny."

Tony spoke for him. "He never knew what hit him or who. It don't matter."

It didn't make him mad at all. He half circled me and stood there a few seconds, then finally said, "You were looking for something, Deep?"

"Same thing you were, punk."

He ignored the sarcasm. "If you were, then you knew Peddle would be away, and consequently probably knew where he was going."

I knew the next step and got there ahead of him. "You can beat my head all day," I said, "but it won't do any good. I was here after Peddle. If you missed him, so did I."

Lenny let the black hate seep out of him. "But I'm luckier than you. After Peddle we were going to find you. Peddle can't hide, at least for long. We'll have him quickly enough. Now you . . . that would have been another matter, but you made it easy for us."

"I'm glad for you," I said.

"You have two choices."

"Oh?"

"You walk out of here quietly, and into a car quietly, and where we take you quietly."

"Or?"

"Don't be stupid. Not you, tough boy. Or we carry you out with a hole in your gut in the right place to slow you down some."

There really wasn't any choice at all. "I'll walk," I said. "Quietly."

We all went down the private elevator to the street, walked fifty feet to the new tan Pontiac and got in like a bunch of old friends. Every move was professionally perfect and no one would ever have caught wise. If they had they would have died on the spot, but with the new regime of hoods it's better not to have trouble.

I sat between the two hoods with my arms folded across my chest, feeling the blunt noses of the two rods against my side. In front, Lenny sat with the driver, his arm across the seat, looking back at me. He was enjoying every moment of it, getting rid of the dirty taste he had whenever he thought of the things I had done to him in the past.

The driver cut crosstown, picked up the West Side Drive and went up the ramp into traffic. They made no attempt to cover their route and that meant only one thing. I was going someplace . . . but I wasn't coming back. I could hurry it or I could wait it out. They really didn't care. The choice was still a singular one. I'd wait it out.

What were the odds? Augie was gone, Cat was gone. Nobody else knew where I was or what I had in mind. This time the mistake was mine for going it solo and it could be the last one I'd make. These were strictly pros now. They

did only one thing. They were assigned to kill, that was all
they knew and nothing could talk them out of it. They'd
shoot as soon as talk and have a hot lunch after they dropped
you in the river somewhere. They didn't think, they didn't
want to think, and to them it was just one more job and
one more dollar.

Lenny turned and smiled placidly. He was happy. I
said, "Hurt, Lenny?"

He raised his eyebrows. "The way you're perched on
the seat. Thought maybe your ass hurt," I said.

Tony snickered again.

Lenny said, "You're going to be fun, Deep."

"Think about it a little bit."

He didn't catch my meaning and his smile came off.

I said, "You're too old for the rough stuff, man."

"Not with you. I've been looking forward to this for a
long time."

"Then you should know better."

Flatly, Tony cut in with, "You think he's got an angle?
He ain't the kind not to cover hisself."

"I think our boy forgot himself this time," Lenny answered.

"You better be sure."

Lenny nodded. "I'm sure. I've known him a long, long
time."

"He's been away a long time too."

"They never change, Tony. You should know that as
well as I do. Isn't that right, Deep?"

I shrugged.

Tony's head swiveled on his shoulders like that of a pray-
ing mantis. He regarded me silently for a long time, then
turned and said to Lenny, "If I was you I'd knock this guy
off right now."

"You're not me, Tony."

"So you'll be wishin' you did. Something tells me."

"I'm telling you to shut up."

Tony grunted something and was still. The one on the other side had taken it all in without batting an eyelash.

We turned off the West Side Highway at the bridge and angled back across town. In ten minutes we stopped in front of a closed restaurant a block away from Yankee Stadium and Tony nudged me with the gun. "Out," he said.

The other one went first, his gun out of sight, but ready. Tony came behind me, the muzzle of his gun steering me toward the door beside the restaurant.

Lenny opened the door and said, "After you."

There weren't going to be many more chances after this one.

But Tony anticipated me by a full half second and the sound of his rod slamming against the side of my head was like that of a board being broken in half.

I could see my feet and they seemed miles away. They were together primly, the toes matching. The feet swam up closer and I saw why they were no neatly arranged. They had been tied like that. I had the sensation I was going to fall forward on my face and slowly I knew why I didn't. My hands were tied behind the chair I sat on with just enough slack to let me hang away from it.

Lenny's voice, sounding very fuzzy, said, "He's coming out of it."

Somebody else said, "Good. Hold that ammonia under his nose again."

Harsh, acrid fumes caught in my throat and I choked, my eyes flooding with tears. I pulled back away from the smell and shook my head. The little gray man sitting in front of me smiled. "Welcome," he said.

I blinked, trying to see him, and when my eyes cleared recognized his face. They called him Mr. Holiday and spoke softly in front of him. He represented the syndicate interest in New York but unless you knew it for sure you'd think he was simply somebody's father. The others sitting comfortably around the room had equal, but different interests. Some of them had been at the meeting the night I walked in the K.O. Club. Now they were watching me in a detached, yet curious way. I was part of the obstacles of their business and had to be handled just so.

"You are all right?" Mr. Holiday asked me.

My head pounded and rather than talk I nodded once.

"Good. You know why you are here?"

This time I said no.

He made a face. "It really doesn't matter. However, you know what we want."

There wasn't any sense playing games. "Bennett's stuff."

"Exactly."

I raised my head and forced a grin. "You can't get it from me. I haven't got it."

Holiday made a quick gesture with his pudgy hands. "That we shall be sure of." He waved a finger over his shoulder. "Maxie . . . please."

Maxie was a big fat guy with forearms like barrels. He walked up thoroughly enjoying what he had to do, looked at me clinically a moment, then whipped the back of his hand across my face. It came too fast to duck and before I could set myself the other one came at me from the other side. With open hands he almost tore my head off and when he stopped my mouth was full of blood from where my teeth were driven into my cheeks and my eyes began to puff out around the cheekbones.

Mr. Holiday said, "You can hear me, Deep?"

I bobbed my head.

"They tell me all about you. They tell me you are very tough. Too, they tell me how you used to make people talk, you and your friend Bennett. You know, naturally what will come next. You will talk or die very, very slowly.

Somehow I grated out, "I know the routine. It won't do you any good."

Lenny Sobel said, "He's lying."

"So? How do you know?"

"Because I remember how the two of them were. I know how they thought. Bennett left everything to this guy."

"Wouldn't he have produced it by now if he had?"

"Listen," Sobel insisted, "you can't tell what angle this one'll play. With Bennett it was cut and dried, but you can't tell with him. They're both nuts. He knows where it is all right! Squeeze it out of him . . . he'll talk."

"Perhaps you have something to say, Deep?" Holiday said in such a kindly way it was hard to believe what he actually was.

"Hell, if you're going to scratch me off, then do it."

"We aren't in a hurry. We have time, but you haven't. It might be easier if you talked to us."

Big Maxie said, "More, Mr. Holiday?"

Holiday held his hand up. "In a minute, perhaps. Maxie here is overly anxious. You should see what he can do with a cigar. Or old-fashioned stick matches. There are certain variations of the hotfoot . . . ah, well, that will come later."

"It won't . . . do any good," I said. I managed to rock back and suck air deep into my lungs. I couldn't feel my hands any more; the rope had bitten in too far and cut off the circulation.

"Obstinacy can be painful, Deep. It will be easier to talk."

I shook my head to clear it but it only pounded harder. "Clue me," I said.

Holiday smiled. "So, we begin. We shall start with the death of your friend. Who killed him?"

Gradually I brought my head up. "You did?"

"Certainly not us. That would be an unnecessary risk to run. Although Bennett was a nuisance factor to the organization over-all, he was better to pay off than aggravate. No, Deep, it was none of us. But maybe you have an idea."

"I had Hugh Peddle in mind."

Holiday nodded and smiled again. "Now there is a good thought. Friend Peddle has been growing in stature. He has been making large demands on the organization. He too was in Bennett's hand. Had he been able to operate freely he could have been even more important, but Bennett held him back. Besides, Peddle is unscrupulous. I'm quite aware of what he would do if Bennett's information were available to him. In fact, do you know what he tried to do to you?"

"Morrie Reeves and Lew James. He hired them to knock me off."

"Right again. Luckily, he contracted for two men we could exert influence over and were able to hold them off a short while. We couldn't take a chance on having that treasure of Bennett's lie dormant somewhere to fall into the wrong hands. We had to know where it was. You know, we even warned Hugh, but he wouldn't take our advice.

"The organization can't afford to lose face. It held still for the bluff and bluster of Benny Mattick because there was a certain possibility that Benny, in his sneaky way, had managed to kill Bennett and uncover that information. In a way Hugh Peddle's action was a challenge to the organization's authority. We wanted you alive until something definite had been established. Did you or did you not have what we wanted."

"Now you know," I got out.

"Not yet. Not for sure."

"So that's why you were after Peddle?" I wanted to keep him talking.

Holiday knew what I was doing but didn't seem to mind. "Hugh must be taught a lesson, one that he'll remember. We had to erase a good man because of him. You shot Morrie and Lew just couldn't be left around while he was wounded. Lew was a junkie and we couldn't take a chance."

"You know what happened to the guy you sent out?"

The smile disappeared. "We heard. Everything they ever said about you seems to be true."

From the depths of a chair Lenny Sobel said, "You're wasting time."

"It's less messy and a lot more quiet if we talk it out."

"I don't mind hearing him scream."

Holiday's tone was soft, but there was an edge there that ended the argument. "I mind," he told Lenny. "Now," he said with a change of expression, "back to you."

I felt all hollow inside, dragged out. I could barely hold my head up. "Too many guys died. Augie . . . Cat . . . it's not over yet."

"You could stop it right now."

"No . . . sorry. Nothing I can . . . say."

"Mr. Holiday?" Lenny's voice had a new note.

"What is it, Lenny?"

He got up, walked to me, grabbed my hair and yanked

my head back. "We've been going about this all wrong. We've been going at it from the wrong end." He slammed my head to one side and let an ugly smile etch his mouth.

"Explain yourself, Lenny."

"The dame . . . Helen."

"So?" Holiday's eyes went from Lenny to me. My stomach turned queasy and my heart started hammering again.

Lenny said, "It's so damn simple . . . so damn simple. She screwed all of us." Lenny was getting a charge out of this now. He watched my face and saw the knife sink in a twist. He could read my mind and started to tear it apart piece by piece.

"Think about something . . . about Helen and Bennett. For two years she's been playing that creep like a harp and that was all he ever talked about. He was so gone over that fluff he couldn't see straight and don't think she didn't know what she was doing. Hell, she did it with me . . . finagled me into more crazy things than I could think of. So okay, I was a sucker too, but not that bad."

"Get to the point," Holiday said.

"Sure. The point is Bennett played up to her, played the big shot so big he had to prove it and gave her the lowdown on why he was what he was. You know how Bennett got on top. He was like a Hitler the way he worked it. Once he was there everybody thought he was good, but *we* know better. A dame could see through him too, so what would he do to show a dame how big he was?" Lenny nodded, intrigued by his own thought. "He'd show her the business. She was going to be part of it, be the Mrs., why the hell shouldn't she know?"

"You're crazy!" I shouted. "She wouldn't go near that

bum! Damn you, just try touching her and I'll kill you, Sobel, so help me I'll kill you!"

"Look who's talking," he said softly.

Mr. Holiday said, "It makes sense. Is there more?"

"Sure, and it ties in very nicely. You know the party Bennett was going to throw at the clubhouse? It was supposed to be a secret, but word got around. That big mouth couldn't keep still about anything. *He was going to announce his engagement to Helen.*"

Words came out of me that I couldn't stop. I called him everything I could think of then slumped back, exhausted.

Holiday shook his head in sympathy. "Quite a violent reaction."

"Sure," Lenny said directly to me. "He was played for a sucker too. Bennett got knocked off before she could actually lay her hands on the stuff and she had to play along with Deep to see if he came up with it."

Holiday stood up slowly, his face resigned. "And did you, Deep?"

Lenny answered for me. "Of course he did. He gave it to the girl to hold for him until he got all his contacts made and take care of the ones who could cause him trouble. That's why he was looking for Hugh Peddle tonight." He laughed deep in his chest. "Hugh owes us a favor. We saved him from getting knocked off." He took my .38 out of his pocket and looked at me meaningfully.

Mr. Holiday walked across the room and picked up the phone. He dialed a number and without bothering to give his name, he said, "I want you to bring Helen Tate to me. Yes, that's where we are. Just a moment. Lenny?"

Lenny called out her address and Holiday repeated it.

He put the phone down and made a motion toward another room. One by one they all filed out behind him and

I heard them mixing drinks and laughing. Lenny Sobel was by far the loudest.

When the phone rang again Maxie answered it, took the message and when Mr. Holiday came back out he said, "The broad is gone, chief."

"He say where?"

"No, but there's a newsie outside the building who saw her leave and knew the guy she was with. It was Hugh Peddle."

There was no feeling in me any more. Nothing.

"Does he know where they went?"

Maxie repeated the question, waited and a minute later said, "The newsie saw him flag a hack. The guy wasn't cruising but was coming into the stand, and the newsie knows him. Says he'll be back pretty soon to pick up some regular trade."

"Tell him to find out where friend Peddle went to with the woman and to call back at once."

Maxie passed it on and hung up.

"It seems as if the Councilman has followed your line of reasoning, Lenny. Things are beginning to look up."

"That bastard!"

"But a smart one. He has ideas about taking over on both ends."

"What are you going to do?" Lenny asked him.

"Me? Nothing. I'll be in a respectable bar somewhere seen by a lot of people. But you, Lenny, that's another matter. When that call comes in I want you to get Peddle. It's your baby and you're in charge. Chances are he took her some place where he can squeeze it out of her."

Holiday stopped there and said seriously, "Deep, you have a big feeling for that woman, don't you?"

I didn't answer, but he knew.

"You know what Peddle will do to her to get the information."

"Damn it," I grated, "she doesn't know anything!"

"No, sucker?" Lenny's face was a tight mask.

"Keep still, Lenny," Holiday said sharply. To me, "If you know where he took her we might be able to help."

Blankly, I shook my head. It was useless, absolutely useless.

"Then," he added, "to go back to the original premise . . . if *you* know where this information is and reveal it, we'll take care of Peddle but let the girl alone. Nothing can hurt us if we have that package."

When I didn't answer he shrugged, "Have it your own way."

Maxie stepped forward, grinning broadly across his moon face. "Chief, you didn't let me try. If I . . ."

"Don't be silly. Deep here is in the same trap Benny Mattick was. He doesn't know a thing. Isn't that right, Deep? Of course it's right. He would have spilled his guts to save that woman if he knew anything. You can see it plain as day in his face."

And there it was. I could be destroyed at any time at no cost. They didn't even have a choice to make now. The fact was simple. I had to die.

Holiday slipped into a raincoat and set a new Homburg on his head. He looked like a banker. He tapped Lenny's chest for emphasis. "I want at least thirty minutes, then do what you want with him." He waved a thumb at me. "Keep Tony and Ed here . . ."

"I don't need them."

"Do as you're told." He snapped. "When Peddle and the woman are located call one of our groups nearest the area and have them move in. I'll see that they are all standing by. They'll be informed to move only at your orders. It doesn't make any difference what happens to either Peddle or the girl, just be sure you come back here with that information. Is that understood?"

Lenny felt surly about it, but agreed. "I'll take care of it."

At the door Holiday turned around and tipped his hat in my direction. "Very sorry about this, Deep. Try not to hold it against us. I know you realize there's nothing personal about it. I really like you."

I wanted to say something smart but there was too much going on inside me to find anything at all to say. I sat there tied up like a dummy and watched Mr. Holiday and his entourage file out the door, until only Tony, his silent partner and Lenny were left.

And Lenny was smiling. He pulled on a pair of gloves and worked them down his fingers.

Tony got up, stretched, and lit a cigarette. "I'm goin' down the corner for somethin' to eat. I ain't et all day."

His partner spoke for the first time then. "Bring me back somethin'," then walked into the bedroom. I heard the bed creak as he flopped down on it.

Lenny grinned wickedly and said, "I've been waiting for this a long time."

I spat on the floor in front of him. "You're too old, you pig. Your heart won't take it."

"We'll see," he said.

Then it began.

CHAPTER XIII

I knew I was on the floor. I knew there should have been pain, but the strange alchemy of the body had started and where the pain actually was I could feel only a throbbing sensation. My head pulsated with each heartbeat like a dam being attacked by floodwaters.

Vaguely, I heard Lenny call out for the other guy to come get me out of there.

He came reluctantly and tested my side with a foot. "Whatsa matter wit' leavin' him here?"

Lenny wasn't the old Lenny any more at all. He could talk it and he could think it, and he could even try to live up to the old days, but time had shrunken him inside and he couldn't take sight of the rough stuff any longer. "Just get him out of my sight and don't ask questions. Put him in the bedroom and stay there with him."

"Crap. I wanted to sack out. After we knock him off we gotta go alla way to that stinkin' quarry in Jersey wit' him. I'm pooped."

"Sleep in a chair. Get him inside."

To drag me he had to untie me from the chair. I could tell when he did it only by the sounds and the way he rolled me around. There was no feeling at all in my hands and feet. I kept my eyes closed, though with the way they must

have been swollen knew he couldn't have told whether
they were open or shut anyway.

He got his hands under my armpits and dragged me across
the room, into the bedroom, and let me flop on the rug
beside the bed face down. With no more concern than if
I had been dead he walked back outside, spoke to Lenny
and made himself a drink.

I tried to move and managed to get halfway over. I
brought my knees up and fought to get my hands under
me. There was no way of telling if I did or not; feeling had
been strangled off from my shoulders down. But the
sudden motion did do one thing. It brought the pain back,
a great, sweeping tidal wave of pain that crashed through
the barrier of numbness my body had set up and closed
down on me like a monstrous pair of pincers. I let go with
a terrible sound I couldn't help and went back on my face
again.

The only good part about it was that the pain reached
my hands and feet as the circulation was restored and although I was powerless to move them much I knew I could
move them a little and it might be enough if I played it
right.

When the guy came back he carried the two strands of
ropes that had held me to the chair, knelt on the floor beside me and tied my hands behind my back. He finished
that, threw a few loops around my feet, knotted them and
got up and laid down in bed as though nothing had happened at all.

Outside Lenny was making himself another drink. He had
two more within a few minutes and between them mouthed
a few curses at the world in general.

On the bed the guy began to breathe slowly, but lightly.
He wasn't quite asleep yet and I couldn't afford to disturb

him now. My hands were still tingling, and though bound, were coming back to normal. There was nothing professional in the rope job the boy did on me and the slight amount of pressure I managed against his efforts was enough to allow me the slightest bit of slack.

I had to wait. I had to lie there and wait while I wanted to explode.

To take the tension off I forced myself to think. I tried to put the whole thing together in my mind and cull out the loose ends and eliminate the mistakes.

Why did Bennett die?

Now *there* was a poser. Alive, he was a threat. He wielded a power that could line up forces the way he wanted them, both political and illegal. Sure, even Holiday admitted that and Peddle proved it by being in the club. There were others involved to make that much certain.

But Holiday had said a peculiar thing. The syndicate didn't really *mind* Bennett. It was easier to take him than knock him over. *Why?*

Back to Wilson Batten then. He laid a finger on Bennett that Helen had known too. Immaturity. Bennett hadn't really wanted much at all! His idea of bigness was really so small they could afford to let him have his way . . . but what he had *was* big enough so that they played it his way all the way and without reservation.

No, the mob wanted him alive. They couldn't afford him dead at all.

Benny? Could Benny have killed him? Unlikely. Benny just didn't measure up to that kind of courage. He would have showed signs of what he had in mind and Bennett would have gotten there first. Or the mob. They'd hit Benny if they knew he was going after Bennett. With a power package, Benny would be more dangerous to them than Bennett by far.

Then there was Tally's death. Hers was the forgotten one.

And there was something else I almost forgot. Whoever killed Tally had killed Bennett and had tried to kill me.

The weapons?

Not a heavy caliber gun and a few well placed, immediately fatal shots the way it had happened to Augie and Lew James and Cat. Not the signs of an experienced pro.

A zip gun and a bottle. A kid's trick. A lousy kid's trick that screwed up the works and started a chain of death that still wasn't over.

Sure, from the beginning it went like that. Take it the way a kid would . . . he figured a guy like Bennett would have cash around and cased his place until he knew the routine. When he knew only Bennett and Dixie were in the house he waited and when Dixie went out, he went in. Bennett answered the door thinking it was Dixie back and there stood the kid.

The kid's first hit, maybe. He pulled the trigger and that's all he had, that one shot. He got Bennett in the neck . . . maybe Bennett staggered and fell, but he wasn't dead. The kid saw that and panicked. While Bennett lay there he got in the elevator and took it down, forgetting to grab any loot.

I could feel the excitement rising in me. I tried to follow Bennett's actions and the kid's at the same time and it began to come out clear.

Naturally, it would have been a local punk, one of the neighborhood gang members. Bennett recognized him and knew where he'd run to and tried to cut him off. He went down the fire escape and through the yards behind the buildings the way I had followed Morrie Reeves after he killed Augie. Bennett had headed for that same alley Morrie had hoping to cut the kid off, all that time holding his hand over the hole in his neck.

And that was as far as he got. The internal hemorrhage killed him right there.

That was where the night people came in. Was Tally coming home from a drunk when she saw him? He must have been close to the mouth of the alley to be that easily seen from the street. I could see Tally in my mind, watch her take in the dead man with one grand look of pleasure, spit on him and walk away knowing that now the fun would begin.

Then Pedro . . . he robbed the body and got off the scene.

But because of these two the picture had changed.

Where was the killer all this time?

Why didn't he run? Could it be that he was seen in the area by Tally or at least thought he had been seen? He shouldn't have killed her; Tally would never have spoken against him. Or maybe that the body was almost lying in the killer's back yard and its very presence would mean an unnecessary danger if anybody put two and two together. A zip gun meant a kid gang. The Scorps?

So the killer carried Bennett back. Bennett was no lightweight, but even a panicky old lady can do remarkable things. He got him back through the rear, took him up the first escape, dumped him in his own living room and left.

A cute detail had fooled the police. Bennett had bled a lot when he was first hit and messed the room up just right. Who would have thought that he had gone out and been returned to the same spot again?

A zip gun. A kid's kick. A simple stupid kill and all hell cuts loose.

Lenny broke a bottle outside. He cursed too loudly to be sober and stumbled into the living room. My head was turned so I could see him through the doorway and when he stopped, cursed again and walked into the darkened bedroom I thought it was over.

"That stinking Knight Owl Club. That whole bunch of stinking jerks!" He took another pull of his drink and yanked the door shut after him.

It was funny, in a way. Just a cellar club from years ago, but the repercussions never ended. They just couldn't get it out of their heads. The K.O.'s dominated their lives, every one who was touched by it.

Nostalgia? Sentimentality? Environment?

It was like I told Helen . . . it was all tied up with the club.

And then the sudden truth came at me like a bomb that grew and grew in size as you watched it and the whole thing burst open in a wild sheet of flame that left you too stunned to do more than gasp.

It was all there. It fell right in place. I had pieces and Helen had pieces and Batten had pieces and Roscoe had pieces and Lenny had pieces and Holiday had pieces and now it was one big whole and it could be too late at any moment to pull the cork.

On the bed the guy's breathing was deep and regular. I tried the ropes, being as quiet as I could. I let my hands hang lifelessly so that no muscular activity would swell them, then began the slow process of stretching and loosening my bonds.

Twice, the man on the bed turned, saying something in his half-sleep, then drifted off again. Each time I waited until I was sure he wouldn't hear the small noises I made, then went back to work on the ropes.

One hand came loose, taking skin with it and I unwound the length of rope from my other and freed my feet. When it was done I lay there until I knew I was all right again, then got up quietly and did what I had to do to the guy on the bed.

He was no trouble at all.

He lay there unconscious, a gag in his mouth, breathing heavily through his nose while I tied him hands-to-feet with a single strand of rope that he wasn't about to loosen. As I finished I heard the phone ring and Lenny move to answer it. He said, "Yeah . . . yeah. I got it," then tapped the receiver bar down, held it and dialed a number. When it answered he said, "Dave? How many you got there? Yeah, six will do it. Holiday call? Okay, then you know you take orders from me this trip. No stay there. I want in on this so don't move without me. Stay in the neighborhood and when I drive up you can move in. Hit Peddle and take the girl alive. We'll do the whole thing inside there where nobody will hear a thing. No, you'll know me. I'll drive the red and white panel truck that belongs to the restaurant. When you see it, start moving in. Just you wait until I get there, understand?" He grunted and slammed the phone back, then let out a little laugh, swirled the ice in his drink, finished it and set the glass down. I heard him walk toward the door. I got behind it. He still had my gun.

The liquor and the light had blurred his sense and his eyes. He must have thought it was me on the bed and supposed the other guy was in a chair asleep. He stood in the doorway chuckling.

"You've had it, Deep. You know why I let you live this long? Because I wanted to let you know what happened to Helen. You know where Peddle took her? To the old K.O. building. You know why? Because she knows that someplace in there is the stuff and Peddle is going to make her come across with it. Only Peddle won't live long enough to use it and neither will the broad."

He had my gun in his hand now and thumbed the hammer back.

I wanted to tell him before I moved that Helen didn't know anything. She took Peddle there because he had already squeezed something out of her. She remembered the last thing I had said . . . that it was all tied up in that damn K.O. Club.

She had a small choice . . . if I had said it then I had meant it. There was a remote possibility that I might show up there in time.

Time.

The gun went off into the ceiling when Lenny's broken trigger finger pulled against it, then his shoulder joint dislodged and the scream he started choked off into a total faint and there was no trouble at all in doing the same thing to him I did to the one on the bed. I immobilized him with the other strand of rope, picked up my gun, reloaded the one chamber and stuck it in the holster.

Feet sounded in the corridor outside and the door swung open. When Tony saw me crouched in the doorway with the .38 leveled right at his nose he shrugged resignedly and said, "I told Holiday he shoulda bumped ya."

"Drop your piece, Tony. Carefully."

He didn't argue. His gun hit the floor, he kicked it aside without being asked and stood there. "You bump the others?" When I didn't answer he added sourly, "Well, I guess that's that. Do it like quick, huh?"

"They're inside," I said.

Tony grinned. "Thanks, pal," he said. It was one pro talking to another. He turned around and waited and when I hit him, folded up neatly. I used his belt and some of the TV antenna wire to keep him put.

The truck was behind the building where it had been backed in from the street. The keys were in it and it started easily. I checked the time on my watch and knew it could be a fast run if I caught the lights most of the way. At that hour traffic was at its lowest ebb and speed could be had, not with the throttle pedal, but by staying in time with the stop lights where neither cops nor cross-town cabs were likely to nail you.

I let the clutch out and eased down the narrow driveway, the headlights like twin fingers leading the way. I switched them to dim. It started to rain and I fumbled for the wipers until I found them and they swept methodically in front of my face.

Time? How much of it was left?

I turned down *The Street.*

The Street.

That's what we always called it. We still did.

In the middle of The Street was *The Club.*

For so many, like a womb. The mother. They came from it, they went back to it. I remembered the key word that had evaded me even though it had been spoken so often by so many people.

Sentimental.

I drove slowly so those watching would see the truck. I couldn't see them, but I knew they were there.

How often I live in the shadows myself, I thought. How many times in all those years I have buried myself in the

night shrouds of a building, waiting, fingering the butt of
a gun to make sure it was ready. In the early days I used to
want to vomit but couldn't, so spat out cotton wads and
sweated, but that was when the gun was new in my hand
and still had that cop's imprint on it.

Sentimentality. It was part of me too. I had kept that
gun for twenty-six years. In its own way it was a symbol,
a reminder. The cop who had worn it got shot down
trying to stop a heist artist about a year later and I never
had to worry after that about him trying to run me down
and take his piece back. It was my first piece of iron and
the only one I ever had or needed. That .38 had been around
the track and back again and had pulled me out of plenty
of tight spots so that we were close friends now. I could
feel it next to me, warm with body heat. The action smooth.
Ready again.

As I passed the building I peered through the rain at the
front. No light showed at all in any of the windows, but
that was no indication of what went on inside. I reached
the end of the block, turned the corner and parked. I cut
the engine, sat a minute and waited, and saw the guy dart
across the street like a wraith and sidle up to the cab of the
truck.

He wrenched open the door, shaking the water from his
head and said without looking up, "Them two gunnies of
his went in there about ten minutes ago. You want to . . ."
He stopped, sudden shock on his face when he saw me.

That was all he had time for. I smashed the butt of the
.38 across his temple, dragged him in the cab and let him
lie there. It would be hours before he'd wake up. Six,
Lenny had said. Now there'd be five. They'd think I had
him stay with me and they would start moving in.

This part I liked. I felt myself grinning when nothing was funny at all.

Henny had done his job well. The back door was nailed permanently shut in the face of fire regulations, convenience and common sense, but it did the job. There wasn't time to force it and if I tried each nail would have sounded a separate alarm.

But there was another way. When the old man used to lock us out for not coming up with the three dollars rent in the days before we were big enough to climb his frame, we used the coal chute window. It was bigger than the others and always unlocked.

And times hadn't changed since.

I slid in feet first on top of a fresh pile of coal, closed the window and got out of the pile with as little noise as possible. My fingers reached for the latch on the bin door, lifted it and I stepped out. It was absolutely pitch dark but I knew every inch of the way.

The light overhead was sticky with dirt and it lit when you screwed it all the way in. I turned the bulb and turned back the years in one second. There was the massive, squat furnace, the asbestos outer skin hanging from it in shreds, but still serviceable. Across the small room were shelves littered with years of accumulation of junk.

Dust had laid a blanket down over everything . . . except in one place. It was where you could get a hand in the bank of shelves and pull them away from the wall.

They still moved easily, the castors under them retaining the age-old grease and not succumbing to rust. The hollow in the wall behind the shelves was the old arsenal of the K.O. members. A butcher knife, two pipe billies and a zip gun with a tape-wrapped frame and four boxes of .22 shorts were still there, mementoes of years past.

But you could see where there had been another gun and somebody had split open a box of shells just to get one out to fit the piece. Somebody in a hurry.

Nostalgia?

The old K.O. Club had something for everybody. Nostalgia was the word. Something always brought them back.

Like, for instance, a person in need of a gun. You just don't pick them up anywhere in New York and if you don't want anybody to know at all, there's always the old K.O. arsenal.

Somebody had remembered.

Nostalgia? The answer again. Buddy Bennett and the way he thought, only with him it was that he never quite grew up. He was still back there in the clubroom days, a man grown and important, but in one respect still a child who couldn't give up the womb. It was his life. It had been his only home. When he had the loot he still couldn't give it up and unconsciously duplicated the womb as closely as he could where he could live as he wished.

But the real thing kept dragging him back. After all, it was the only real thing he ever had, his only true *woman*, the one who birthed and nurtured him and in his mind she had birthed and nurtured me too. We were, in effect, brothers from the same mother.

It was to her that he came to place his offering in her womb where he knew only I would look since we both had the same mother.

He was wrong, but he didn't know that then.

I found the place we had used, just the two of us, to secrete our most precious things, the things we considered important then. I kept my rod there, the metal and leather oiled and wrapped so it was always nearly perfect. He had kept his things there too.

You took the cement block out. You reached down in the hollow.

And there it was.

Something like a lover's packet of letters. Some were letters. Some were pictures. Some were photostats of documents and some were the documents themselves.

Not much, but enough.

He could run an empire on them.

He had.

I put them back for the moment, then went out into the main room of the old club. Just one big room with a curtained alcove at one end spotted by a jumble of chairs and boxes with a radio in a special place because at one time it had been a status symbol.

In the corner a phone. The ultimate status symbol for a clubhouse.

Had Bennett recognized the symbolism?

Overhead the floor creaked. I paused, thinking the faint strains of a scream marked the quiet.

Easy. Don't rush it. It has to be done right. I repeated it to myself. There can't be any chances. The odds are wrong and the cost too high to pay.

I picked the phone up, dialed Information and asked for Roscoe Tate in a whisper. She gave me the number, I dialed it and when it had rung a few times the ringing stopped.

Quietly, I said, "Roscoe?"

"Yes?"

"Deep."

There was no smart talk now. He had seen the carnage at the rooming house and without having seen the papers I knew he had made the most of it.

"Another scoop, friend."

"I told you I don't need any favors."

"You'll like this one."

"Go on."

"It's over, little man. The gang is all busted up. In five minutes they'll be taking each other apart and the ones who are left over will be on hind tit because I have the works. I found Bennett's power package and I'm going to wrap those miserable pigs up like in the old days and watch them cry."

"Where are you, Deep?"

"At the old clubhouse. Grab your pencil and come along. It'll be the biggest story of your life . . . the one you always wanted to write. That old gang of mine. All one big obit."

"Deep . . ."

"But come easy," I said. "They got Helen upstairs and first I got to shake her loose." I was grinning and he knew it. "Maybe you'll get your wish, kiddo. I may not make it, but somebody had better be here to take care of Irish."

Before he could answer I hung up.

I made one more call. I couldn't afford to buck the odds. Alone I might get part way, but that was all. Both sides wanted Helen and if there was any doubt she'd be better off dead than alive.

The operator gave me my number, the one who answered gave me another to call and I got Sergeant Hurd at home. I said, "Don't talk, just listen," and gave him the poop.

His voice was as cold and as nasty as he could make it. "Stay alive, Deep. I want you all for myself."

I laughed. "But just in case, hardman, I could still beat the crap out of you anytime."

"Stay alive, Deep," he said, "if you got the guts to."

I was certain now. It was a scream from upstairs.

I put the phone back and yanked the .38 out, thumbing the hammer back. I went up the stairs into the narrow vestibule and almost tripped over Henny. He was alive, but blood flowed from a gash in his head. He still had a flashlight in his hand and I took it from him, tested it and snapped it off.

The picture was fairly clear now. Hugh Peddle had come in, sapped Henny and probably made a quick tour of the place with Helen. When she couldn't come up with anything, he called for his boys. They'd be in bad shape, but still more the type to squeeze a woman than he was. Peddle was ruthless. He could give the orders, but personal involvement when it came to putting heat on somebody was another thing.

I went up the stairs and like the last time, felt the notch Bunny Krepto had carved out with his switchblade the night before Petie Scotch had killed him and ran my hand over the break in the post at the top of the landing just like in the old days.

Think.

Think.

Five are looking for three. Possibly seven guns and if Peddle packed one, eight.

There was a scream again and I spotted it. They were on the top floor and I could hear the terse, whispered commands that came through the walls. The others had heard it too.

Only now the edge was mine.

I had run the course more often than they and knew the twists and turns. I knew the way the wall angled back at the landing, and how you could get through the window to the part of the old fire escape that had never been torn down and if you wanted to take a chance, could climb up.

A core of steel still existed under the rust otherwise it never would have held. I got to the window I looked for, and strangely enough it eased open after all these years, or else Henny had been a better caretaker than I assumed.

They had her in that big room, sprawled out on the floor, her raven hair spilling out over her shoulders and her dress high above the waxen smoothness of her thighs.

Hugh Peddle wouldn't look. He stood to one side examining his fingernails while the guy, Al, the guy I had shot in the arm, was standing spraddle-legged over Helen, his arm in a sling and he was enjoying everything he was doing. He had a rag wrapped around his good hand so he wouldn't carve up his knuckles and a few feet away the other guy whom I hadn't seen before watched him with obvious pleasure.

I laid the sights of the .38 on the back of Al's head and held it so I was sure of the shot. He had his foot ready and was going to put the boot to her in another second and the instant he moved his brains would come out through the front of his face.

My finger curled around the metal, I started the squeeze, already had Hugh and the other one in my peripheral vision to kill next, when somebody yelled and Hugh spun around toward the door at the far end of the room and said, "Who was that?"

"Knock that light out!" Al told him.

Hugh reached the switch, flipped it and threw the place into total darkness.

They had locked the door, but it gave under a barrage of shots. I heard Hugh yell hoarsely and run toward the far end. He wasn't a pro like the other pair. They snapped off a couple of fast shots, scrambled for the protection of the furniture and stayed there.

I put the gun back. I didn't waste any of the seconds I had left. I went crabwise across the floor, found Helen and dragged her backwards. By then the ones outside had hit the front entrance and knocked the door open. Somebody was yelling for a light.

She tried to fight me until I told her to be still. She recognized my voice and slumped with the sheer relief she felt.

Together we inched forward on the floor, got to the break in the room and cut around the angle of it.

Behind us the roar of gunfire was a steady thing and bullets were slapping into the walls and skipping off the metal things. Somebody began screaming and wouldn't stop.

I said, "Are you hurt badly?"

"No. They had . . . just started to . . . really hurt me."

"We have to climb down a flight and bypass the action."

"All right."

So I helped her out above me, guided her feet into the rungs and hoped the steel would hold until we reached the level below.

Luck was on our side this time and it did. The gunfire above abated, then started again. Feet slammed down the stairs and we flattened out against the wall. When they passed we followed them down, stopped at the first landing, cut back to the rear where the other stairwell went down to the basement and held it while I listened.

A voice far above us was yelling that they had them and the shooting stopped abruptly. Another voice found Al, the other and Peddle, and they were dead. Somebody wasn't quite sure about one and there was another shot and everybody laughed.

When they couldn't find Helen they made a circuit of the room and suddenly realized what had happened, only they thought she had done it all by herself. There was a sharp order and feet began pounding down the stairwell.

I grabbed Helen and we made the last run into the old clubroom.

Outside on The Street sirens began their unearthly howl, coming closer and closer and it was almost all over.

They never quite reached us. They stopped when they heard the squad cars and being pros, knew the score. They scrambled for a way out, but being pros, knew that the cops would have that end covered too.

We huddled there in the pale light that drifted out of the coal bin, heard the cops smash their way in and listened while the shooting started again. They were pros up there and were going as far as they could because there was nothing else to lose. On the top floor were three dead men and the wheel would turn on all of them because of it. All they could do now was take out their hate on society until they were dead or their bullets were gone and hope they died first because the death the law prescribed was, in reality, more horrible than dying with a cop's bullet in your gut.

Helen said, "Deep . . . ?"

"I didn't lay a gun on anybody," I said.

Her hand felt for my face, found it and pulled it down to hers. Her mouth was cold and I could feel her tremble under my hands.

"Please, Deep . . . I don't understand."

"Look . . ."

"Hugh Peddle came. He made me tell him what you had said."

I squeezed her shoulder. "I know what he did."

"He thought I knew."

"He was wrong."

A riot gun roared into the night, tearing things apart. Whistles shrilled and somebody shouted orders directly above us. More sirens were coming in now, surrounding the block.

Like an air raid, I thought. *Death a few feet away.* You *huddle together in a dungeon of a cellar and listened to death upstairs.*

I said, "I called Roscoe. He should be watching this. It'll make quite a story."

"But . . . he hates you."

"He hated everybody, kitten."

She felt the change in my voice. "What do you mean?"

"Tell me, were you engaged to Bennett?"

Helen pushed back, stared at me, her eyes searching for my meaning. One side of her face was all swollen, but she was still beautiful. "No, Deep," she said. "He asked me, but I told him no. You know what I was trying to do."

"He didn't know that, kid. He thought he had you. He was going to let all the boys in on the big secret that he was going to ask you to marry him."

"But how could he . . ."

I interrupted. "He never grew up. Remember . . . he still thought like back in the old K.O. days. To him, if you stayed close, you were his."

"He was mad! I never . . ."

"Did you tell Roscoe he asked you that?"

"Well, yes, I did, but . . ."

The firing grew more intense. A section of ceiling powdered and came down like snow around us.

Very slowly, almost dreamlike, Helen turned and looked up at me. Her eyes were large, dark. She caught my intimation but couldn't believe it. "Not Roscoe," she said.

"Your half brother."

She put the seal on it herself. "No . . . he was my father's stepson, thanks to an earlier marriage. He really wasn't my brother at all."

The last seal. It was done.

I said, "He was always in love with you."

"Oh, no." Her face buried itself against my chest and I knew I had to tell her then.

"It was Roscoe, kitten. It was bad enough he hated all of us, but long ago I had you and he knew it. He wanted you himself and because I had you it warped his whole life. He didn't stay here for any reason other than to direct his hate at the things that took you away from him.

"Me, I was long gone. Psychos learn to redirect their hatred and you even helped. He could take almost anybody, but never me or Bennett. When Bennett proposed to you he flipped. He really flipped. It was like having me there again. It was the old days. He went all the way back to the crazy hatred of the old days."

She still couldn't understand. It was too big for her.

"He went nuts, sugar. Roscoe went absolutely nuts. All he could do was think of how he could kill Bennett and he reverted to those old days himself. He had no gun but knew where we used to keep them. He got down here and opened the arsenal and found a zip.

"You know, if the gun hadn't been there he might have come back to normal. He might have realized what he was about to do, but there was still a couple of pieces and some ammo in the old spot behind the shelves and he pulled one out and loaded up.

"Bennett was killed at night. Early. Not a normal hour for a kill at all. It was before ten when most pros haven't started out yet. Roscoe went up there, popped Bennett who was waiting for Dixie, ran for it and passed the alley where Bennett had run. See . . . he hadn't killed Bennett. When he knew Bennett followed him he had been running toward his own sanctuary . . . Hymie's deli, which was still open. The thought that anybody would connect them scared him and in that frenzy all psychos get, did the impossible . . . carried Bennett back to his apartment and dropped him."

I nodded.

"That's what happened. He was out of his mind. He was a full-fledged madman. He was something else, too. He was a catalyst. He did something terrible to the world he lived in. He ousted Bennett but reintroduced me. He started things happening, instituted forces he never thought existed, and in his madness, never gave a true thought to what he had done."

Somebody opened up with a Thompson upstairs. There was another scream. They were firing from the full perimeter of the building now and the sound of guns and cars and voices was a cacophony of sound that made music perfectly suited to the city. It was a moment of moments.

"He was a madman at the first kill," I said. "Not the second."

"What?" Her voice sounded small.

"Roscoe killed Tally, Irish."

"He . . . no!"

But she knew I was right. "He wasn't mad the second time around. He knew what he was doing then. I scared him when I told him that Tally spat on his corpse. I scared hell out of him when he heard about Pedro bone-picking. All he thought was that they had seen him run by, or perhaps pack the body back. He got to Tally with the only weapon he had at hand—a bottle. He nearly killed me with the same thing.

"That's what I overlooked. It was a simple kill to begin with. An amateur kill. Only the prize involved was so big I gave other people credit for smoking up the trail. It would have been worth the try."

She said, "But Tally . . ."

"He wasn't a madman then, kid. He was covering his tracks. I'll give you odds that before long a small Mexican named Pedro will turn up dead someplace with his head squashed in or his throat cut. Roscoe knows the turf. He could run anybody down he wanted to. He's as worldly-wise as I am and playing it just as cute and now his back is to the wall."

From the darkness of the coal pit Roscoe said, "Not all that far, Deep."

We couldn't quite see him, but we could hear the madness in his voice. Out of the shadows his hand protruded and in it was a gun if you could call it that, and that you had to because it had already killed two people. Long ago Bennett had killed Spanish John with it and not too long ago Roscoe had killed Bennett with it and now there was another bullet left and it was going to be in me. I had to come first because when I was done it would be an easy job to handle Helen and not too hard to explain away the kill, especially when you were a madman and knew the ropes too.

He stayed right there, the gun leveled at my head with a strange, deadly precision that most amateurs don't ever attain but a madman might.

There was death all around us now. Upstairs the hammering had slowed, become intermittent, then suddenly stopped. There were feet pounding up the stairs . . . voices shouting back and forth, counting the dead.

It had to come.

It came very close by too.

Somebody had found the door that led to the old cellar club.

The K.O.'s.

Us.

Remember us? We were the big ones.

Time again, the one factor that enveloped us all. There was just so much of it. He could shoot me and club her to death. No trouble. It would stick. He was smart. He could do it, explain it off and get a story out of it afterwards. I thought of all the ways he could do it and knew how easy it would be.

She said, "No matter. It's over now, isn't it?"

Back there in the darkness I knew he was ready. The gun was small, but the tube of it was something I could look into. I could even imagine the deadly little .22 nestling there ready to puncture my skull the way Bennett had designed it to, knew the chances of a misfire were as remote as missing your head with a hat. The little man was crazy cool and had already thought out the answers and I was his only obstacle left.

There were only seconds more and we all knew it and Helen squeezed my forearm not really knowing what to do, the pure love she felt wanting to throw herself in the line of fire, but holding back because I pushed her back and let Roscoe play it all the way out.

"You're dead, Deep."

His voice sounded strained when he said, "The end of the trolley ride, Deep."

"Is it?"

"You're like all the rest. You paid your nickel, you get the ride."

"I guess you heard what I said."

"I heard it all."

"You're nuts, Roscoe."

"Let's say I was. As you stated, now I'm protecting myself."

"You're still nuts."

"No more."

"Sure you are, small man. You forgot the big point."

He paused, then. "Go on."

"The trolley ride."

"So."

"It's my nickel. I can get off wherever I please. Remember your simile of the trolley?"

And he did. Like the amateur he was he came screaming through the door with the same gun he had killed Bennett with only this time it was for me and while Helen was screaming with a partial realization of what was happening I drew and fired and shot Roscoe Tate through the right eye and his brains spattered all over the clubhouse walls.

He seemed terribly shrunken in death, a little guy who had nursed a big hatred for those for whom he'd held a big envy too long. It wasn't the bullet that killed him. It was *The Street*. He had been killed a long time ago and never knew it.

Roscoe Tate had died when he tasted fear, and instead of spitting it out like the rest of us, forced himself to swallow it. He was killed when he let a revengeful satisfaction chain him to The Street and twist his guts until the explosion came.

Helen's hands were pressed against her mouth, near hysteria making the cords in her neck stand out like wires, pressing her face out of shape until her face had an animal look. Blood squirted suddenly from her lip, staining her teeth a bright crimson.

But she wasn't looking at the mess on the floor. She was looking at me.

There were more police whistles blowing upstairs. More voices and ominous sounds. Somebody threw the door open and a splash of light beamed down into our cavern, searching, yet reluctant to press the issue.

They knew where we were!

"You had to do it," she said. "*You had to do it!*"

I frowned at her, looked at the gun in my hand and slammed it back into the holster.

"Helen . . ."

Eyes that hysteria had held wide too long suddenly washed themselves with tears and she dropped her hands to her sides in abject helplessness. Her lip was swollen from where she had bitten it and very softly a sob caught in her chest.

"You had to go and kill him, Deep. *Why?*"

"Helen . . ."

I could barely hear her voice. "Why didn't you kill me, Deep? It would have been easier that way." I tried to stop her, but she went on. "You killed him, but you should have killed me. In a way you really did anyway."

"Please, Helen."

She shook her head, the futility of the whole tragic moment caught in a single gesture. "What is there to say, Deep? I had to go and love you. I had to fall crazy in love with you. I should have known. All this senseless disregard for life and peace and happiness was part of me in the beginning too . . . but I got away from it. I hated it. I never wanted any part of it . . . I even tried to stop it. Then I came back because of you."

She stopped me with a wave of her hand when I went to speak. "It's no good, Deep. It's over now. I would have waited for you forever if I had to. You were my man. You knew that, didn't you?"

I nodded silently.

Her eyes were bright with tears and she touched my face. "I didn't care what you did. I didn't care what you were wherever you came from because you were mine and I was yours and when it was done we would be together, even if it was for a little while and we were very, very old."

I said, "I didn't come from so far away, Helen. Not in distance. Just in time."

She listened, but didn't truly hear. "But you spoiled it, Deep," she told me. "You committed the one crime there's no turning back on. You did the one thing you said you wouldn't do. You threw all our love and our promises to the wind when you killed him."

The tears spilled from her eyes, shining wetly against her cheeks. "If you could have been . . . just anybody . . ." she hesitated a second before she spoke . . . "it wouldn't mean anything. It wouldn't be so bad. But when you're part of something like . . . all this . . ." she stopped, sobbed and pressed her hand to her mouth again.

You could hear them coming down the stairs now, being very careful.

". . . then it's over. There's only death now. You committed the one crime there's no turning back on. There's no possible defense. You're one of them, Deep, and when any one of them kills, the law kills back.

"And now the law is going to take you and when you die, I'll die too. That's what you did. In one second you threw away everything we ever had. You should have let him kill me. You did anyway. You should have let him."

A voice called for a riot gun and there was a shuffling on the stairs. Others were standing by, ready to fire and step by step they started down.

I said, "Helen . . . I love you."

She smiled, sadly, her eyes a little cloudy with tears that had a bitter sting. "I know," she said, "and now it's too late. There isn't even any hope left and we had so much. So very much."

Behind us they reached the bottom of the stairs.

Then I grinned, real big, and in a brief moment she

knew that because years ago two kids had decided to split the world between them didn't mean that both of them had to keep the pact and that somewhere along the line the worse one had found out that to hop off the trolley wasn't the way to abandoned hope. In that one brief second she knew the reasons and the answers for a lot of things.

They were there, guns out, all of them. Sergeant Hurd in front with the riot gun and the rest with service revolvers. There was only a second left now.

In that one scant second, that tiny particle of time, she had a glimpse of that flash of gold pinned to the wallet I held in my hand when they all came up behind us and lowered the guns and knew. *She knew.*

Sergeant Hurd said, in a tired command voice, "Nice going, Lieutenant."